A LITERARY
SMORGASBORD

A LITERARY SMORGASBORD

MEMOIR, FICTION, AND POETRY

MIGEL JAYASINGHE

To my dear friend Abey (Kirti)
with Love and best wishes for
a happy, healthy and long life
from Mahinda (migel)

To order additional copies of this book, contact:
Xlibris
800-056-3182
www.Xlibrispublishing.co.uk
Orders@Xlibrispublishing.co.uk
792718

QUIRKY BIO

My parents couldn't believe it when I left secondary school without getting into the one and only University of Ceylon. At school, my teachers insisted that academically I was within the top ten percent. Unfortunately, they steered me towards science and maths, with an eye to better prospects for future employment, when clearly my strengths were in Arts subjects.

Disappointed, I still managed to get a job as a junior clerk in the Civil Service in Colombo, the capital. Scribbling on files all day, with a monthly salary barely enough to pay for my board and lodging, I was disconsolate.

One day, as I was walking to my workplace from my lodgings nearby, I went past the door of an astrologer, or, as the logo insisted, a palmist. I felt that the word soothsayer would more aptly describe the services of this man. On my way back from work, seeing the palmist's premises still open, I walked in.

I remember that the man called himself G. Henry. A middle-aged man dressed in local garb, then coming into fashion as the 'national dress', he was seated behind a table, with an alarm clock and a writing pad before him. Mr Henry looked at the clock, presumably to ascertain the time, and began to draw lines or diagrams on the writing pad with a ballpoint pen, directing me to sit in the chair opposite.

Mr Henry explained to me that he had to mark the heavenly positions of the planets at the exact time when I entered his office. He was able to read my future from the position of the planets. But then, he also took a close look at the palm of my right hand.

'Writer!' he said.

He then went on to explain that my future had to do with language, words, and letters. I already knew that my literacy was much stronger than my numeracy. Most of my fellow schoolmates' aspirations had been towards prestigious employment such as doctor, lawyer, accountant, engineer, and at the least, teacher. How G. Henry was able to pluck out 'writer', from thin air, as it were, was indeed amazing.

My best subjects at school were English Language and English Literature. I always won the class prize for English. I wrote short stories and articles for the school magazine, and throughout my school career, I contributed to the Children's Page of a local newspaper. However, becoming a published author and taking up writing as a full-time career, I surmised, was but an unrealisable dream, especially when the couple of local newspapers I applied for work as a reporter or sub-editor turned me down flat.

Years later, I immigrated to the UK, but did not make it as a writer. Instead, I gained qualifications in psychology as a mature student, and struggled to make my way in that field. Now a pensioner, I scribble poems on a pad and wonder whether I would live long enough to be recognized as a 'writer'.

CONTENTS

OVERLAND

These events occurred more than a generation ago, 45 years ago, to be exact. The world has seen some changes since. I have changed too. I am a different man to what I was then. How exactly, I don't know. Writing this may help me understand how ageing and experience has helped me to order my life in a structured narrative; how I faced (or avoided) the challenges along the way. The world's events are a backdrop to my story, with nation-states, ethnic groups, and ideologies vying for dominance, or at least, for expression of their own identities and separateness. I don't think I am writing a memoir, although everything I write here is from memory. I did not keep records, or a diary, and I will be the first to admit that memory can play tricks. My only promise to the reader is that I do not deliberately falsify or alter facts to fit any premises I seek to advance. However, the selection of facts and events that I dwell upon here do stem from my interests and preoccupations which are unavoidably mine alone. Hopefully, by the end of these pages you would have some idea of what they are, and whether they merit being expressed in so many words.

Essentially I am here describing an overland trip from Cambridge, England, to Bombay (Mumbai), India, by car, during the summer of 1974. It is impossible to imagine undertaking such a tour today, crossing the violent and embattled regions of Iran, Afghanistan and Pakistan, to reach India overland. Yugoslavia does not exist as a country anymore. It has been fragmented into several smaller states. I made the journey in the company of two young ladies, mere acquaintances, with whom strangely or otherwise, I never developed a close relationship. They were of course, between them, close friends, seemingly inhabiting their own universe. Perhaps to be expected from a certain type of Cambridge girl? Indeed, I do not even remember their names. For the purpose of this narrative, I shall call them Mary and Jane. Mary was the one who owned the Vauxhall Estate car, who persuaded me to be the co-driver and male escort for the trip. The latter role was thought to be essential, especially when it came to travelling across the so-called third world, mainly Islamic states. It was Mary who put the notice, a postcard, up on the Cambridge Alumni's Union Notice Board, asking for someone (male) to accompany her as co-driver to travel to Bombay, India. Although I was not a Cambridge graduate, I was granted the privilege of honorary membership since I was accorded access to the University Library as part of my work role, as a research assistant, with the Industrial Training Research Unit. There was no mention of a return from the trip or of a time scale for the journey, at that stage. There was a telephone number to call. It had occurred to me that such a journey would be fun and perhaps even cheaper with petrol costs shared, than any other form of travel. I, of course, wanted to continue my way by train and ferry to Sri Lanka, my country of origin, once we had reached Bombay. As an immigrant, I felt that there was nothing more I could achieve by remaining in the UK, and thought I was ready to return to my native land. Mary was quite agreeable to our breaking up and going our separate ways as soon as we reached Bombay. She then mentioned Jane as the only other passenger, a Cambridge undergraduate friend of hers. Mary herself had completed her studies a few years back and was employed in an agricultural laboratory. She would resign her job by the end of the month. She met me at my lodgings in Milton Avenue, a flat I was sharing with two young men who were connected with the intellectual life of Cambridge in different ways.

Mary was nearly my height (5' 10") and robustly built. She made it clear from the first that there was not going to be any hanky-panky. Although she had acquired British nationality, her parents were Norwegian doctors who had served the British Raj in India. Her childhood was spent there with ayahs and servants at her beck and call, but was later sent to boarding school in England. It was nostalgia that beckoned her to revisit India. She asked me why I wanted to return home to Sri Lanka for good. I told her that I came to England with great hopes for my future, but even after 11 years, I didn't think I had got very far. The previous November, for the first time in my life, I was able to secure a research assistant position in Cambridge using my

London University psychology degree gained more than 2 years ago. Until then I continued to be engaged in all sorts of menial work from dish washing to van driving. The research assistant position was only a temporary one-year contract with ridiculously low pay. I felt I could do better back in Sri Lanka, although I had learned that things were not all that sanguine under a left-wing government presided over by the world's first woman prime minister, Mrs. Bandaranaike. I would try to sell, or donate the few books I possessed to charity, and would have only one suitcase full of clothes and toiletries to take with me. I would sell my battered old Austin mini for whatever I could get. I had to admit that I had no savings at all. Mine was very much a hand to mouth existence. Mary had worked out that a little over a hundred quid each should get us safely to the sub-continent. I felt that I could sell the old car for about that figure.

As you may have gathered, at the time of embarking on the idea of an overland trip I was still a single man, although I had already reached my 38th birthday. I was about three months shy of my 27th birthday when I immigrated to the UK from the former British colony of Ceylon, now Sri Lanka. I had survived 11 years and 2 months struggling to make something of myself in the host country. Most of my compatriots of roughly my age, who came over to the UK at that time, had never been in regular paid employment in Sri Lanka after leaving school. I am sure the British thought of us as a source of cheap labor and issued us with 'priority vouchers', entitling us to enter Britain. We were all educated in the English medium and spoke tolerably good English. Unlike most of the others, I had held a responsible job as a Sub-Inspector of Police for nearly five years, before I resigned over a dispute with a superior. During a period of about one year after leaving the Police, I served as a commissioned officer (Lieutenant) with the Ceylon Volunteer Force, the equivalent of the Territorial Army in the UK. Except for very short periods when mobilized for duty, I was not on regular paid work before my embarkation to Britain. At the time I was not looking for a steady job as I had been planning to emigrate as soon as practicable. I could only afford to sail on the Messageries Maritime ship SS Vietnam, in one of the cheapest, multi-occupied cabins like most of my compatriots. I remember the disappointment of one of the French crew, when he came over to assist me with my luggage, just one suitcase, and realized that I was only a poor migrant like the rest. Since I was somewhat taller than my compatriots and had the military bearing of the recently trained soldier, I must have appeared to him a better class of passenger.

I left secondary school with only a few GCE O' levels, although I had spent two, indeed three years in the Sixth Form, when I was allowed to take the University Entrance examination twice in succession. Much to my parents chagrin I, the eldest of four, three brothers and a sister, was unsuccessful in gaining admittance to the then one and only University of Ceylon. My parents, poorly paid 'vernacular' (native tongue) teachers living in remote parts of the country valued the advantage of an English education in the metropolis for their offspring. However, they could barely afford to send me, the eldest, to Colombo, while the others attended schools in various provincial towns. A malnourished child living in unregulated private boarding houses in the capital, I was forced into being a bookworm unfit to take up any kind of physical activity including athletics or sport. My interrupted schooling meant that I stopped being concerned with school subjects requiring any systematic study, but took to frequenting the British Council, the US Information Center, and the Municipal Public Library, for intellectual stimulation. This meant that I just scraped through or failed subjects other than English, for which however, I never failed to win the class prize. I regularly contributed sketches and stories to the College magazine and the youth pages of the local English language newspapers.

Although Ceylon gained independence from the British Empire on 4th February 1948, as a member of the Commonwealth, in the 1950s, we felt ourselves still beholden to the inherited British education and administrative system with the language of the state apparatus and commerce remaining English. I was still a schoolboy when Queen Elizabeth II opened the Ceylon parliament during her visit in 1953. I was recruited as a special policeman for crowd control and therefore able to see at close quarters the beautiful young queen and her consort, the Duke of Edinburgh. I had wanted to join the police, but as a physical weakling with no athletic accomplishments, I felt it was out of the question. There were college cricketers, and school record holders in various athletic events, who were sought after to fill officer vacancies in the armed forces and the Police. Rural folk, physically fit, but with hardly any qualifications could join up as privates and constables, but at our level, we were thinking of joining as ensigns or Sub-Inspectors of Police. The latter became officers in charge of small, rural police stations after working at provincial headquarters and learning the ropes as assistants to the Inspector in charge. Promotion to the ranks of gazetted officers (A.S.P., S.P.) was also held out as a likely prospect.

As the next best thing, I sat a country-wide examination selecting clerical staff to man government offices, and was successful in getting into the Auditor General's Department as a grade 3 clerk, in Colombo. During my last year at school I had tentatively taken up swimming and now was able to join the Kinross Swimming and Life Saving Club. They had a tiny clubhouse, no more than a shed situated along the seafront in Bambalapitiya, a seaside suburb of Colombo. Along with other place names like McCallum Road and Campbell Park, this was a reminder of the Scottish community lording over us during colonial times. However, there were no longer any Scots left on the island, and the only white-skinned Kinross members were from the Dutch burgher community, a small influential group who opted to remain as Ceylon citizens until, in time, they made their way to Australia, Canada and Britain.

You may not believe it, but I learnt to swim from an illustrated book on swimming, which I had received as part of the Sixth Form Prize for English Literature. I was also occasionally and haphazardly helped and coached by members of the Kinross Club whenever we gathered at the Ceylon's only Olympic-standard swimming pool at St Joseph's College. Now, I could afford a better class of private boarding house and was able to eat well. I began to build up my physique and started taking part in swimming competitions, representing the Auditor General's department in Government Service inter-departmental meets. Although I never mastered the Butterfly stroke, I was able to be placed at least third in several freestyle, breast-stroke and backstroke events and gained a few certificates. As a member of Kinross, I took part in the annual open two-mile sea swim. My first attempt was a failure in that I did not yet have the stamina to complete the course. On two consecutive years following, I completed the two-mile sea-swim but was not among any award winners.

Now I began my search for a more exciting and better paid career. I did not get into the Navy when they advertised for inductees as sub-lieutenants. My lack of proficiency in Physics let me down. Still, working with figures at the Auditor General's was boring. I applied to join the Police. It took more than a whole year for them to complete checks into my background. My parents, grandparents, uncles, aunts, all came under scrutiny. At last they called me for interview. Obviously, the members of my extended family were all law-abiding, respectable citizens. I was now 21 years old. On invitation, I made my way to the Katukurunda Police Training School. There were quite a large number of young men applying for 27 positions as trainee sub-inspectors of police. I was told that the selection process was repeated everyday of the week. To be a sub-inspector of police was an eagerly sought after calling – the best paid and secure job for someone with no qualifications other than a few GCEs. As a first step, everyone was given a pad of paper and asked to write an essay on a given topic. I remember the topic of the day as something relating to road safety. In half-an-hour, I wrote a well-argued essay, which the Assistant Director of Training, a Dutch burgher gentleman named Brohier, deemed to be a model essay. He turned away the rest of the applicants, but not before urging them to read my essay and reach that standard in case they thought of applying again.

Not yet 22, following a series of exhaustive physical checks, I remember reporting for the six-month residential course of intensive training at the Police Training School on 1ˢᵗ April 1958. There were 27 of us, while the constable cadres were in their hundreds. There were also 3 trainee Assistant Superintendents of Police who were Arts graduates of the University of Ceylon. Wearing Khaki uniforms we paraded and drilled under the careful eye of a Regimental Sergeant Major with the voice of a kettledrum. We learnt to shoot with .303 rifles and were instructed in the use of automatic weapons like .38 and .45 caliber revolvers. We also learnt the law of the land, including the country's Penal Code and the Criminal Procedure Code. Weekly tests in law revealed my scores to be higher than that of the trainee Assistant Superintendents. While the ASPs learned to ride horses, the sub-inspectors were taught motor-cycle riding. The motor-cycle was the essential vehicle of conveyance for a sub-inspector. The ASPs rode their horses only on ceremonial occasions, and used cars for day-to-day transport, while the police constables rode push-bicycles, or walked while carrying out their official duties.

In spite of my lack of athletic prowess during my schooldays, I surprised myself by taking part in Tarzan-like jumps over ditches, running road races while keeping up with the pack, and walking across two palm trees rigged with a rope bridge about twenty feet above ground. If you could not accomplish these feats you were out on your ear. I also shared the record for rifle shooting from a standing position, alongside the avowed best shot in the group, who had been a school cadet. I had never before even seen a rifle at close quarters until I joined the police. However, what pleased me most was being chosen as the leader of the debating team composed of three trainee sub-inspectors and arguing my case against the three trainee ASPs. This took place in the officers' mess one late evening, and the Director of Training who had already left through the open main door after setting up the debate, was compelled to remain standing listening to my oration with obvious surprise and satisfaction. On the strength of this I was chosen as the mess secretary, but found the chores unappealing that I didn't come up to scratch and was labeled 'lethargic' and unmotivated.

At this time, there was very little inter-communal strife which was later to mar the political landscape of Sri Lanka for decades to come. We had Mohammedans, Tamils and Sinhalese who were from different religious faiths such as Islam, Hinduism and Buddhism, with converted Christians belonging to both catholic and protestant persuasions. The fair-complexioned Dutch burghers who had dominated the police and the armed services under colonial rule did not think much of the 'brown sahibs' now in power and slowly began to move to other shores where they could blend in without being conspicuous by their skin color.

Athletes, Boxers, Cricketers and Rugby players were the elite of the Training School and although my more modest swimming prowess was utilized to get some trainee constables to pass their required swimming test of 50 yards across the lake, I was never amongst the really 'sexy' S. I.s (S.I. for sub-inspector). I had been a loner at school anyway, and although the term didn't exist at the time I may have been seen as a nerdy eccentric. Unlike some of the others, I had even yet to have my first heterosexual experience. To my dismay I had to reveal this during discussion of the indictable offence of rape defined in the Penal Code, where 'penetration' was a relevant factor. So, although I was never going to win the best all-round trainee award, in the end, I managed to pass out within the top ten, in order of merit.

As a Probationary Sub-Inspector of Police I was posted to a Provincial Headquarters where, at the large red-brick building of the Police Station in the centre of town, a senior Inspector of Police was in charge with about fifty men under him. There were also two Assistant Superintendents and a Superintendent above them placed in overall control of the province. There was a sub-inspector with a sergeant and two PCs under him who took over the traffic control duties of the provincial town. He had a motor-patrol car allocated to him. There were also a number of Land Rovers driven by police drivers to convey officers and men to sites of criminal inquiries and to places requiring crowd control and public safety. All the sub-inspectors at the HQ, numbering about four, had motorcycles, allocated to them. However, it must be said that most places that the police were required to visit in the course of their duties were not accessible by motorized transport. Trudging across rubber and tea plantations at night proved to be the greatest hazard. Unless you wore Wellingtons, not practicable all the time, your feet were liable to be attacked by leeches, which sucked your blood and stuck to you - yes, like leeches.

Returning to the point where I was negotiating with Mary as a possible co-driver for her and Jane's trip overland to Bombay, Mary wanted to know whether I would be happy to sleep in the estate car with the front seats lowered while they slept in a small tent. We could not afford the luxury of staying the night in hostels or hotels. It could be different when we got closer to India. With feminism at its height in fomenting inter-gender animosities, I dared not even hint at a lesbian relationship between the two girls. There really was nothing at all overtly sexual between them, as I discovered, once we started the journey. Remarkably, it appeared that all three of us were abstainers with no thoughts of sex on our minds throughout the itinerary. There was so much happening on the roads that we probably had no other thoughts than how to get to the next point of the journey safely.

Mary looked around my room in the Cambridge flat and appeared to be satisfied that I would fit the bill. I had been in the flat only a few months and the two co-occupiers were happy to let me go at the end of the agreed rental month. They could always find someone else. I set about trying to sell my old car. This was more difficult than I thought. Cards on corner shop windows didn't get any results. A girl-neighbor indicated some interest, but the male 'friend' whom she invited to inspect the car appeared to be an ex-army bloke demobbed straight after Britain's Kenyan Mau Mau adventure. He glared at me and got me to drive the car while he sat in the passenger seat. He then got down and asked me to put the hand-brake on while he pushed the car from behind with all his might. The car moved, and that was it – there was no sale.

When I told Mary my woes, without another word she took the car off my hands and within days gave the £100 I had asked for it. She merely told me not to worry and I didn't think it necessary to ask questions. Mary was in charge, she was the owner of the car we would be travelling in, in good condition, she assured me, although not entirely new. By then, I had only completed nine months of my one-year work contract. When I told my bosses about my plan to travel back home overland, they made no objections. I had been assisting senior occupational psychologists in their action research activities at various locations, while also spending a great deal of time at the Cambridge University Library researching and extracting notes from books and journals to substantiate a thesis being put forward by the co-director of our Unit in his forthcoming book.

At that time I discovered a newspaper advertisement for an occupational psychologist position in Lusaka, Zambia. All I had was a BA (Hons) degree in psychology and the nine months work experience at the Industrial Training Research Unit based at Cambridge. To my surprise, not only did they respond to my application, on learning that I was about to leave Cambridge for good, they advanced the interview to accommodate me. The founder of the Educational and Occupational Assessment Service in Lusaka, Dr Mary Allen, who had then retired, presided over the interview panel. On hearing that

I was a recent member of British Mensa, Dr Allen turned to the two Zambian gentlemen on the panel, and asked them to look no further. However, I politely asked them to await my decision until after I had reached Sri Lanka. Again, most surprisingly, they agreed. These were very early days for occupational psychology in the UK. In the USA the equivalent, Industrial/Organizational psychology was well established. However, there were senior expatriate British psychologists working in Lusaka, and I was told that I could learn the ropes from them.

I still possessed a Sri Lankan passport and had to obtain visas for all the countries we had to pass on our way to India. I visited all the Embassies, High Commissions and Consulates that Mary had listed for me to obtain the visas. I got them all in time except for the one for India. The man at the desk at Bush House, Aldwych, insisted that I should get it at the border between Pakistan and India. He assured me that there would be no problem. If my memory serves me right, we were to travel across Holland, Germany, Austria, Yugoslavia, Bulgaria, Rumania, Turkey, Iran, Afghanistan and Pakistan before we could reach India. Our estimate was that it would take a month, driving only during the daylight hours.

I do not remember the exact date but it was probably mid-August 1974, when Mary, Jane and I, set off from Cambridge for the overland tour to India. I had met the two girls together at the Cambridge Union premises and they could not have been more dissimilar. Mary was large, feisty and gave the appearance of being in control, whereas Jane looked thin and worn-out and had very little to say for herself. She kept in the background throughout the journey. Before we set off, they never invited me to their homes or lodgings. I was not introduced to any parents or relations who may have been interested in their venture. Was there nobody in the background who was curious to know whom they had picked as their co-driver? Apparently not. Meanwhile, my bosses were gracious in wishing me good luck on the journey and even took me out to lunch at a restaurant in Ely. I remember exploring Ely cathedral before lunching on a fresh trout decorated with a daisy stuck in its gills.

Mary drove the Vauxhall car until we reached the Hook of Holland after crossing over by ferry. It was then that I discovered that Mary and I would be the only drivers. Jane did not drive. Once you got used to it, it was not too difficult to remember to drive on the right hand side of the road. The only time it was difficult, was when setting off early in the morning after resting for the night. Of course, Mary and I would always remind each other. I remember one of our earliest overnight stops was at a campsite in Vienna. I found sleeping in the car comfortable enough. The girls spent the night in their green, canvas, two-person tent.

We must have kept changing money every time we crossed a border, but strangely enough I do not remember these transactions. I remember having to produce our passports and getting them stamped. These formalities were subject to more and more delays as we continued to travel eastwards. There were questions probing the purpose of our journey. Even after an hour of grilling, we were always allowed through. We ate frugally, mostly resorting to sandwiches made by ourselves at the early stages of the trip. Whether Mary had a stove for hot water for us to make tea or coffee, I do not remember. Perhaps we did.

Until we reached Turkey we were able to use launderettes to keep our clothes clean. An occasional shower at a campsite was also possible. I cannot recall how we managed to keep ourselves and our clothes clean while driving across countries in the Middle East and Asia. I distinctly remember bathing in both the Black Sea and the Caspian Sea. I believe it was near the Black Sea that our car got stuck in the sand. No amount of revving in first gear made the vehicle move forward. The nearside rear wheel kept rotating as well as sinking ever deeper in the sand. Finally, a castaway wooden plank came to our rescue. I laid it lengthwise wedged against the problem wheel and pushed, while Mary drove the car across it to safety.

In either Bulgaria or Rumania we were stopped by the police and fined on the spot for speeding. This was on a rural road with hardly any other vehicles for miles on end. Mary was philosophical about it. She said that foreign travelers were targeted this way to line either the coppers' pockets or to enhance the state revenue, or both.

As soon as we reached Istanbul, the former Constantinople, we realized that we were no longer in Europe. The Blue Mosque was a sight we could not miss. The girls had to wear hijabs and cover their ankles with long black drapes before they were allowed to enter the mosque. My old pair of jeans posed no problem. Sight-seeing was secondary to our main purpose, which was to get ourselves to India as soon as practicable. In Turkey, there were no campsites that we could find unlike those of Europe. I got the idea of driving up to rural police stations and trying to make friends with the coppers. In spite of language difficulties I managed to get across to them that I was an ex-copper. Once or twice we were allowed to camp on the Police Station premises itself and treated to warm goat's milk first thing in the morning.

Once in a rural location in Turkey, we were allowed to park on the premises of a restaurant where we were expected to have our evening meal as a return gesture. Apart from the two girls sitting with me at table, I do not think there were other women eating at the restaurant. I felt that we were being closely observed by a few men sitting at a nearby table. While we were tucking into our kebabs, we were approached by one of the waiters and asked whether we would join the group of men. He pointed to an impressive looking Turkish gentleman and said that he was interested in one of the young ladies in our group. It was quite clear that in the Middle East someone of Mary's sturdy and ample physique would have been seen as the epitome of feminine pulchritude. The man obviously had his eye on Mary. It was entirely possible that the men may have conjectured that the girls were on display and could be hired for sexual purposes. We declined as politely as we could. We pleaded extreme tiredness after several days of driving. We hurriedly paid and left the restaurant. Behind the restaurant, in a parking area where we had parked the car, the girls set up the tent and turned in for the night. I slept in the car as usual.

In the dead of the night I was awakened by a 'swoosh' sound, the sound of air escaping from one of the tyres. I sprang up clutching the kitchen knife I always kept next to me, and as I opened the door with an oath, a man, possibly the waiter who sought to proposition Mary, dropped something and ran away. Immediately I noticed that the man had removed the tube valve of the front nearside tyre, and that the air was escaping, now more slowly. I woke up the girls, and as soon as Mary saw the flat tyre, she calmly brought out the foot pump and began inflating the tyre.

'I know we agreed not to drive at night, but this is an exception, we are leaving now'.

I did not expect either Mary or Jane to object. They quickly took the tent down and we were away the next moment. We were careful to ascertain that nobody was following us. So, they wanted to have us at their mercy, perhaps begging for help, and very likely it would have been Mary's fate to sacrifice her virtue to get us all out of their clutches alive. However, we quickly got ourselves to the Iranian border without further mishaps.

The checks at the customs border with Iran were exhaustive. They checked the log book against the chassis number of the car. They asked questions about our final destination and the route we intended to take to reach it. Finally, they let us through. As we reached Tehran, we decided to camp out near what looked like a public park. There were no other tents visible, but nobody objected to our putting up the tent next to the parked car in what must have been a public place. There were kids playing football and other games in the park. Gradually a small crowd of youngsters began to gather around us.

'You got two wives?' one asked me in heavily accented English.

'No, No!' was my unthinking and instinctive response.

Mary was busy fixing the tent, while Jane was carrying a bowl of something or other. The lad who had just spoken to me now approached Mary, and I did not know quite what words were exchanged, but I saw Mary sending the youth reeling backwards with a resounding blow across his cheek.

'Come on, we are not staying here one more minute', I bundled the tent and contents hurriedly into the car. The girls sensed the danger they were in, and we made a hasty retreat while the youngsters stood at a distance making threatening gestures and noises. It did not take us long to find an ostensibly safer, but lonely place alongside the highway.

We ate quite a lot of watermelon on the way. These were cheap and sold on various spots along the highway. It was easier for me to answer a call of nature anywhere we stopped by the roadside, but it was a bit more difficult for the girls. We were still able to find the shelter of large trees and shrubs by the roadside and the pair became quite adept at posting me as the look out and perform their natural functions without being disturbed. Then at one point in our journey, the car's brakes failed. I cannot remember whether it was Mary or I who was driving. Somehow we managed to bring the car to a stop by the roadside, and waited for assistance. We considered ourselves lucky in that very soon we found ourselves being towed to a rural garage. It was rather late in the day and the car would only be attended to the following day. While we were wondering where to pitch our tent and the delicate matter of my sharing it with the girls, the owner of the garage came to our rescue. He offered to put us up at someone's spacious house for the night.

Although this time we were completely at their mercy, so to speak, we did not think of it as a ploy for some nefarious activity. The mechanic and his friends, who had now gathered into a small group, appeared decent and well-meaning. We accepted their offer. We had heard that it was a custom in the middle-east to provide shelter and alms to strangers in this way. We were driven to a large house with a central courtyard. There were womenfolk there who agreed to make sleeping arrangements for Mary and Jane. I was allowed to sleep on a mat on the floor in one of the verandahs leading into the courtyard. But before all that, there was to be a feast. Quite unusually for a Muslim country there were alcoholic drinks, although I do not remember whether these were bottled and imported stuff, or perhaps some home-grown hooch. About six or seven men, plus the two girls and I were seated round a large centrally placed carpet or mat in a spacious room. Each person had a banana leaf for a plate on the floor in front. Rotis were piled up in the centre. There were also cooked meat, either mutton or lamb with a rich gravy in large bowls. I do not now remember what the conversation was all about but I remember it being very lively. We were being urged to eat more and more - which we did. There were sweetmeats for dessert. It must have been very late when we went to bed. I mean to our respective mats laid on the floor.

It was early dawn when we left the next day. Obviously the car had been repaired already, and Mary rushed around waking me and Jane up to get us ready for the day's travelling. It occurred to me that Mary was keen to get going before most of our hosts were up and about. She was not keen to prolong our stay and having to endure elaborate goodbyes. The roads were not as well maintained as those in Europe, and our progress was hindered by having to take several detours. The situation changed for the better when we reached Afghanistan. Mary had been told that the road crossing the capital Kabul on the way to Pakistan was built in two stages, part constructed by the Americans and the other part by the Russians. It seemed strange that the cold war enemies had contributed equally to the construction of a splendid highway in a remote corner of the world which was to be the envy of the neighboring countries of Afghanistan.

To me the winding passage through the Khyber Pass was an unforgettable experience. Much later, when I stood in front of the Grand Canyon, and traversed it by bus, I had a similar feeling of wonderment at nature's grandeur. My regret is that I was not able to behold the majesty of the Bamiyan Buddhas before their destruction by the Taliban when I still had the chance. Communication with the Afghans was more difficult than with the Turks or Iranians as it was almost impossible to find people capable of speaking even a few words of English. However, I found it even more vexatious to communicate with Pakistanis and Indians, as seeing my brown skin and Asian features they would begin to address me in Urdu, Hindustani, Malayalam, Tamil, or any one of 100s of other languages native to India. I could only present a blank face and perhaps be thought a deaf-mute.

In Pakistan, I only remember spending some time in Lahore. The rest is a blur. At tea shops when they discovered that I spoke no local lingo, and sensed that I was not really one of them, they tended to become distant and even obstructive. Parading around with two white women, the locals first took me to be a 'playboy'. When looking for places to stay the night, they would stop me and ask me pointed questions. My eagerness to deny any sexual intimacy with the girls evoked only disdain. They saw me perhaps as a servant employed by the women, or worse, a eunuch. Unlike in the countries we had already traversed, in Pakistan and India, it was difficult to stop ones' personal belongings being pilfered. One had to be always on guard. Among a few other things, I remember losing my one and only pair of sunglasses at one point where we had stopped to make inquiries about the route.

We crossed the Pakistan-India border at a place I remember as Waga. I now realized why the man at the Indian High Commission had waived aside my request for a visa. It could be obtained at the border, but at a price. Mary was adamant about not pandering to the local custom of greasing the palm of the young man at the border control. However, he had his revenge by designating a couple of items of Mary's belongings as requiring customs duty to be paid before they would be allowed into India. Although a receipt was handed over, Mary had her suspicions about the legitimacy of this transaction. However, there was nothing much we could do about it.

This area being part of the Punjab, there were Sikh temples and we were put up for the night without charge at one of them. The man in charge had a register where all who crossed the border at Waga in either direction had entered their names and left comments in a variety of languages. I too remember writing something in Sinhala, my mother tongue. The man showed me a number of past entries in that language. For the first time since our travels began the three of us slept alongside each other on mats placed in an open area at the top of the building very much like a solarium. After a restful night's sleep we woke up to the dawn chorus of colorful and exotic birds.

I may have been driving a bit too fast for Mary's liking on the excellent Afghan roads, that she was adamant that she should be the only person to be driving her car for the rest of the journey. She asserted that she was more familiar with India and the driving conditions there than I was. She had a point, especially when she started mentioning Dak bungalows as possible venues for us to break journey and stay overnight. These were very similar to what was known as Rest Houses in British Ceylon.

However, in spite of Mary's concern for the car, and her careful driving, the Indian Grand Trunk Road proved too much of a hazard to the health of the car. It busted a suspension spring when we had just passed Delhi. We had been able to visit a few sites like the Taj Mahal and were able to bathe in the river Ganges if not the Yamuna. Again, sight-seeing was secondary to our purpose. None of us even possessed a camera, and was far from being the leisurely tourist. Our aim was to get to Bombay fast, as we were approaching the limits of our individual travel budgets. However, getting the car repaired was no easy task. The garages did not have genuine Vauxhall spare parts. The mechanics who finally undertook to do the job had to make do with whatever they had to hand. Somehow they got the car in drivable condition again, although the result was far from being a smooth drive. I do not remember exactly what the reason was, but the last few miles to the YWCA in Bombay, almost opposite the fabled Taj Mahal Palace Hotel, was undertaken by taxi. On getting down from the taxi, Mary and Jane quickly said their 'see-you-laters' and disappeared inside the YWCA Building. Having bought a few trinkets to take home, to my dismay, I realized that I had run out of Indian rupees. Meanwhile, drawing attention to the lack of parking facilities, the taxi driver and his 'mate' were urging me to pay up quickly so that they could get away. Towards the cost of the rest of the journey, for me to get to Sri Lanka, I had set aside a five pound note which I thought would exchange into enough rupees for the purpose. While I was fumbling with my wallet and searching for rupees, the taxi drivers 'aide' saw the £5 note and called out;

'Give me that Sir, and I'll bring you change'.

Foolishly I handed him the £5 note. I waited about half-an-hour before I realized that that was the last I would see of what was left of my money on that trip. I was certain that I still had some money in my Midland Bank current account at Cambridge, but in those days there were no Midland Bank branches in Bombay for me to be able to access it.

I must have looked a pitiful figure to Mary, when I sought her advice, that she kindly allowed me to stay a couple of nights at the YWCA at her expense. Someone told me that I could ask for charity or at least a loan from one of the Christian Charitable organizations in the city. I made an appointment to see a gentleman in one of these organizations the following day. It was within walking distance from the YWCA. The next morning as I was walking towards the charitable organization, whom do I meet but the taxi driver's helpmate walking past me pretending not to notice. I was so incensed that I rushed at him and grabbed him by the collar.

'Where's my money?'

'Sir, … sir', he was squirming.

I had seen where the nearest police station was and I had no hesitation in pushing and pulling the man in that direction. Soon, I was relieved of the burden of a citizen's arrest by the arrival of a young man in khaki uniform. I told him the story. I said that I did not mind him taking the equivalent of one British pound off the fiver for the taxi ride, but I needed the rest – badly. Twelve or more years back, I would have looked like that youthful officer in khaki. I could not help but notice that our uniforms 'back home' were smarter. An instance of irrelevant one-upmanship, when it mattered least, it now occurs to me. We were now at the police station compound. The officer listened to the story of the accused. Perhaps they were speaking Hindi. I didn't understand a word.

'I'll deal with this rascal', the policeman assured me, in English. He then slapped the guy a couple of times and chased him away with a kick to his backside. That was instant justice. There was no word of recovery of any cash. I realized then with dismay that there was nothing more to be gained in hanging around that police station. Indeed, I could have made matters worse for myself by giving way to an impulse to strangle the policeman. I made my way to the charitable organization without further ado.

The European, (I could not exactly place him in terms of nationality) took my details and asked me how much I needed to get home to Sri Lanka. He took a photocopy of my passport. I asked for GBP 10.00. I assured him that the money will be repaid from funds I still had in a bank account in Cambridge, UK. Since I was paid monthly in arrears, there was bound to be some money deposited at the end of August, for the work I had done until my departure. It was now mid- September. However, I needed to check with the bank before I made any payments. Having already paid off the room rental, I was sure to have been left with cash I normally use for living expenses. I took down the name and address to which the check should be posted. I was glad to get my hand on a crisp £10 note and immediately ran to the railway station to change it into rupees and buy a third class ticket to Madras.

By this time, I was in a sorry state, health-wise. I had developed a rather delicate stomach and had to be very careful of what I ate. Obviously, a case of Delhi belly. Even worse was a sore I noticed on the top of my left foot. How the bruise got there in the first place, I had no idea. I was wearing flip flops and that made it slightly easier. With a sore and bruised left foot, I found it impossible to carry or even drag my suitcase to the railway station from where I was lodging. However, it was not difficult to find a man to carry it to the station. I could not say my 'goodbyes' to Mary and Jane as they were not to be seen anywhere at the YWCA when I departed. Knowing Mary's reluctance over farewells, I thought she had made herself scarce deliberately. I was vaguely aware that Jane was planning to return to the UK by plane soon enough, but that Mary had no plans to return for quite some time.

In the carriage I entered on the Madras train, there was standing room only. Having delivered the suitcase, the porter began arguing about the two rupees and few paisas I paid him. Even while the train had started moving he was swearing and gesticulating at me through the window. Obviously he wanted more, but I needed what little money I had to get me from Madras to Dhanuskodi and then by ferry across Palk Strait to Mannar in Sri Lanka. There was to be another train ride from Mannar to Colombo on the 'Yal Devi', the express train from Jaffna to Colombo Fort. The last leg of getting to my brother's house about ten miles inland from the capital, had to be done by taxi. I was in no condition to contemplate a bus ride. However, I was not sure where I could find the money for the taxi.

Even with all my careful handling of the equivalent of ten British pounds in the local currency, I found that I had very little cash left when I reached the site of the ferry at the southern tip of India, to cross over to the northern coast of Sri Lanka. The guy who carried my suitcase on to the ferry had to be paid off by kind, since I hadn't much cash left. He asked whether I had any nylon shirts in the suitcase. I gave him my best blue nylon shirt and thanked providence for the invention of synthetic fibres. Now I was left with just enough money for the train ticket to Colombo.

Soon after the train started to move, it was not a ticket inspector, but a police inspector with a couple of PCs who began checking passengers' belongings for contraband. The inspector may have sensed that I was not the type to be looked upon with suspicion and began to chat with me in a friendly way. I was able to tell him that I had been a sub-inspector in the late 1950s and was able to compare notes about noteworthy events and people in the police from that period. I felt confident enough to broach my problem and of my situation about the lack of funds for the taxi ride home. I took his card and said I would send a check immediately on my reaching home, when he offered me a higher denomination Sri Lankan rupee note.

What do I mean by going home? While I was living with my parents, we never had a permanent home. My parents as government service teachers were transferred every few years from one remote village to another both in the 'up country' and 'low country' areas of Ceylon. When I was small and they were both assistant teachers we lived in rented accommodation. I say 'we' but for most of my young life I had been farmed out to paternal grandparents or to uncles and aunts. As the better qualified of my parents, my mother became a head teacher of a girls' school when I was about nine, just before the youngest in the family, my sister, was born. We were then allocated government quarters, built in such a way, that they were attached to, and part of the school building. My father remained an assistant teacher until the last few years before retirement. Usually he would cycle daily to another school several miles away from my mother's school. The 'home' that I now referred to, belonged to my younger brother, who after a university education had achieved a senior position in the higher echelons of the civil service. He had built the three-bedroom house with a government loan. He was still a bachelor with both parents, now retired, living with him.

I finally made it to my brother's house in Talawatugoda, about ten miles inland of Colombo, one day in the second half of September 1974. I had more than enough rupees left to pay the taxi. My mother was very tearful and started attending to my 'war' wounds immediately. My brother, whose pet name was 'SET' formed by the initials before his name, still owned the Morris Minor he bought on joining the civil service all those years ago. Luxury items like cars were no longer imported. A man of few words, according to him, the country's economy was in dire straits. English was no longer the official language and the country no longer attracted foreign investments. My father would queue up early at the local Co-op to buy a loaf of bread before the bread ran out. Fresh fish and meat were luxuries only available at black market prices. It was very unlikely that I could find a worthwhile job anywhere in Sri Lanka given the prevailing conditions.

Within days I had communicated with the Government of the Republic of Zambia expressing my willingness to serve with the Educational and Occupational Assessment Service in Lusaka, as an occupational psychologist. The acceptance came almost by return of post. Although my brother SET was to remain a bachelor until his untimely death following early retirement later, I took my parents concern about my remaining single more seriously. I have described elsewhere how I got involved in a whirl of social events and found my lifelong companion, my wife, whom I took with me to Zambia days after our wedding in January 1975.

Following my request, the Zambian authorities sent us two air tickets to Lusaka. My contract of work was to be for three years starting mid-January 1975. We were put up at the Ridgeway Hotel, Lusaka, until they found suitable premises for us to rent. I established contact with my bank in Cambridge and having got down a cheque-book was able to repay all debts contracted in the course of my overland journey to my country of origin. With a 3-year loan from my employer, I was able, for the first time in my life, to buy a brand new car, a Fiat 127, assembled in Zambia.

More than a decade of suffering, hard graft, and living in limbo in Britain, had been worth it at last. My wife, Sue, found work as secretary to the American head of the World Health Organization in Lusaka, working almost until she gave birth to our son just before Christmas 1975 at the Lusaka General Hospital. There was a vibrant expatriate community of professional people from practically all over the non-communist world, although the hand of the Chinese was very much visible even then, in the form of joint trade ventures and cheap imported goods.

The world has changed so much and so have I. Pseudonymous, Mary, Jane, - and me - our paths have never crossed since that fateful, never-to be-repeated overland journey from Cambridge to Bombay, forty-five years ago.

***

RUDDERLESS LIVING

I was born a decade before the end of the second world war at the height of the British empire in a remote village in colonial Ceylon. My parents were both 'vernacular' teachers employed by the state. Vernacular was the word used to distinguish native languages from the Imperial language, English, just as it was used by the Romans to distinguish Latin from all other languages used by subjects within their empire. I and my three siblings spoke only Singhalese (our native tongue) at home. I was the eldest, and as such carried the burden of setting an example to the others, which made me the recipient of many harsh physical chastisements, especially from the mother. Academically better qualified, a trained teacher, she was the dominant partner in the marriage, having risen to a headship well before my father...

At the age of seven, I was required to walk seven miles over a dirt track to the nearest English school run by a Catholic seminary. Only the last one mile or so was macadamized. There were other boys who did this daily trek, but they were much older than me. As I remember, at least on one occasion when I fainted from fatigue on my way back from school, I had to be carried home by a benevolent passer-by.

Since my parents were transferred from one village school to another, in disparate parts of the country every four or five years, I was soon placed in a boarding school in the hill capital Kandy. Between the ages of ten and twelve, I attended another English school, this time at Kalutara, a seaside town. At the age of 12, the year we gained independence from the 'mother country', Britain (1948), I managed to pass the entrance test to a prestigious Buddhist 'public' school in the capital, (Ananda College, Colombo 10). Since there were no vacancies at the college hostel, I was boarded at a succession of private homes close to the school. Invariably, I had to share a bedroom with at least one other lad. All my belongings were contained in one suitcase, or 'trunk', which was carried back home at the end of every school term. Within a year or so, the government passed legislation providing universal free education. My parents did not have to pay school-fees anymore, but my board and lodging costs were not insignificant.

By this time, I had acquired a good grasp of the English language and became fond of reading whatever books I could lay my hands on. The school library was well stocked with literary works including the English classics. Even though we hardly ever listened to English programs on the radio, the library shelves were stacked with British journals, including the 'Listener'. We listened to Singhalese and Hindi pop music, on local radio broadcasts. One of our daily newspapers, the 'Ceylon Daily News' reproduced the British 'Daily Telegraph' cryptic crossword, which I invariably struggled to complete.

By the time I reached the Sixth Form, reading Darwin, Freud and Marx gave me license to see myself as a 'free thinker'. When the Principal tried to persuade me to undertake a Buddhist religious observance ('*Sil*'), I refused, which I later realized had cost my place at the one and only university in the country at the time (University of Peradeniya). This was in spite of my winning the class prize for English every year. I was lucky enough to have excellent teachers of English. Two of them became my friends for life. I am still in touch with one of them, a retired lady teacher in her late nineties, now living in Paris. I was not all that good in science subjects in which I trailed behind others. Indeed, several of my classmates eventually ended up as professors of Mathematics, Physics, and Chemistry, both at home and abroad. As for me, my only accomplishment was contributing short stories and articles to the annual college magazine. Occasionally, the ' Ceylon Daily News' also published my sketches and stories in a weekly page set apart for children's contributions.

Being a weakling physically meant that I could make no contribution to sports or athletic activities at the college. When I left school with only a few GCE O' Levels to my name, the best paid and glamorous job one could get was as a Sub-Inspector of Police. These positions were much sought after and required applicants to face very stiff competition. It took me over three years to build myself up physically and acquire swimming certificates, and, confidence to enable me to enter the Police Training School as one of 27 trainee sub-inspectors. Since leaving school, I had worked as a clerk (civil servant) at the Auditor General's Office in Colombo 7. I was almost 22 when I joined the police. It took that long because of the background checks into my extended family of grandparents, aunts, uncles and cousins scattered around the island.

I surprised myself as one of the best shots at the Police Training School using the .303 rifle. I regularly beat the trainee Assistant Superintendents (three graduates) at weekly tests in law, mainly based on the country's Penal Code. I also became the leader of the debating team. I believed I had more than made up for my lack of sporting and athletic achievements at school.

After completing the six-month training course, I was placed as a Probationary Sub-Inspector at a provincial police headquarters. I soon became an Assistant Officer-in-Charge and was sent as Acting O-I-C to smaller stations in the province when the OICs were on leave or on training for higher positions. At one of these remote stations, I took full control of a murder investigation, apprehended the absconding murderer and later (much later, after I had left the Police), proved my case in Supreme Court, entirely based on circumstantial evidence. Having survived rigorous cross-examination by defense lawyers, I was highly commended by the judge who said that he believed it was a loss to the Ceylon Police that I had left the service However, much earlier, when I apprehended a powerful individual with possession of a vast quantity of cannabis plants, this proved to be my undoing. I was immediately transferred to the Colombo Headquarters for a desk job in Traffic and Information. I did not realize that my new superior (Superintendent) had been suspected of involvement in corrupt practices and placed there, away from direct contact with the public, as a precaution. According to subordinate staff, he had expected a backhander from me before he would confirm me in my post at the end of the probationary period of three years. He delayed my confirmation by six months for no ostensible reason. I confronted him, and thoroughly disgruntled, handed him my resignation.

The bureaucracy surrounding police resignations were such that it took nearly a year before they finally released me. Soon enough, as one of the collaborators in a failed coup attempt against the elected government, the 'Super' was retired before his time. I later learnt that he was able to prove a certain percentage of white (European) ancestry, according to the ethos of the time, and was allowed to settle in Australia. After the failed coup, the government required officers to man the country's reserve army urgently, and I was selected for a commission in the volunteer force (equivalent to the Territorial Army in the UK). Another six months of square bashing and studying military law, I was a 2nd Lieutenant ('one-pipper') in the Pioneer Corps. This was 1961/62.

However, part-time soldiering did not satisfy me. I now considered immigrating to the UK, to work, but also with the ulterior motive of returning to my studies and improving my chances in life. I applied to the British High Commission and was awarded a 'priority voucher' to enter Britain.

Along with two of my former schoolmates I embarked on a voyage to the UK on the French passenger ship SS Vietnam in March 1963. We deliberately avoided one of the worst winters of the UK in recorded history (1962). We disembarked at Marseilles after 14 days of sailing via Suez and took the night train across France to reach Calais the following morning. We took a cross-channel ferry, being sick, and to a man throwing up the hastily eaten pork pies overboard, before arriving at Folkestone on a grey and gloomy afternoon. An express train then disgorged us at the Victoria Railway Station, London, as evening fell. It was on 30th March 1963.

Five years of menial work, washing dishes, factory assembly, van driving, night security, ice-cream selling, postman, and the like, was my lot while I acquired GCE A'levels through self-study, while attending evening classes extending over a period of three to four years. My subjects were; English Literature, British Constitution, and Economics. I had to overcome another hurdle before I was allowed to enter London University to read psychology for a BA (Hons) degree. The requirement was for a GCE O' Level in a modern European language. I attended evening classes at the West London College in Notting Hill for a year, before I got that qualification in French. Since I did not have science subjects at GCE A' Level, my qualification would not be designated a B.Sc. although the curriculum and the final examinations were the same for both the BA (Hons.) and the B.Sc. However, I had to pass an internal mathematics paper before I was finally declared suitable to read psychology as a full-time student at the University of London, Goldsmiths College (1968-1971).

It took a while before I was finally awarded the annual £400 grant covering the three-year period of my degree studies. I was attracted to psychology mainly because of the narrative and literary charm of Freud and Jung's writings; although at the time I could not have articulated it as such. I found reading popular journals in psychology, in some way, therapeutic. I was therefore disappointed by the dull 'experimental' and statistical treatment of the subject that the course at Goldsmiths provided. It was the heyday of behaviorism and what went inside one's head, the 'black box', was totally ignored. The word 'mind' was taboo and anything relating to consciousness was dismissed as being 'metaphysical', a term of opprobrium to almost all psychologists of the time.

Meanwhile, I found that I was always short of cash after paying the weekly rent for my digs, that I had to ration my food intake and visits to the launderette. Soon, I found a uniformed job as a part-time security guard where I could work the whole of the weekend at a factory-site eating stale sandwiches and drinking coffee from a Thermos flask, and, earning a mere 'fiver' (£5) for my pains. Unfortunately, this restricted the time available for serious study at the College Library as well as the London University Senate House Library. I left university with just a Lower Second class degree. Such a degree, I soon found to my dismay, was almost worthless in the job market.

After a short period of work as a proof-reader at a publishing house, I returned to work as a van driver, not only because it paid better, but because of the freedom for me to be away from the put downs and backbiting I found endemic in an office environment. I delivered anodized metal work to householders in Edmonton and Tottenham in North London, who returned the finished (assembled) products through me back to the factory. While engaged in this job, I had the opportunity to read the London evening newspapers. In those days in London, there was an 'Evening News' in addition to the 'Evening Standard' still much in evidence today. The 'Evening News' carried items designed as IQ tests over a period of a few weeks and I discovered that I was quite adept at doing most of them correctly. So,

I applied to take the supervised IQ test and was recognized as falling within the top three percent of the population in terms of general intelligence. I soon found myself a member of British Mensa.

Mensa paved the way eventually for me to become a Chartered Psychologist. Once, I was invited to the Blackheath home of the then British Mensa President Victor Serebriakoff for lunch. I was also one of the participants in a televised program on Mensa presided over by David Dimbleby in 1973. The Belbins (Eunice and Meredith) directors of the Industrial Training Research Unit in Cambridge saw me on the program, called me up, tested me further, and offered me my first job in applied psychology as a research assistant. Much later, in the 1980s with a Masters degree in occupational psychology from Birkbeck College, I could proudly call myself an Occupational Psychologist with Chartered status. Much of my professional work since, has been in rehabilitating those disabled and disadvantaged in the world of work, with whom I obviously had a close affinity.

In August 1974, I left my job and digs at Cambridge, sold my little old Austin Mini for £100, packed everything else I possessed in a suitcase, and left with two Cambridge girls in a Vauxhall Estate owned by one of them on an overland trip to India. (I have written up this exploit in slightly altered form and length under different headings. The longest version of over 5000 words was serialized by a local freebie newspaper 'The Coastrider' in 2009). Before I left Cambridge, I had appeared before an interview panel which selected psychologists for the Educational and Occupational Assessment Service, a government department in the Ministry of Labour and Social Services in Lusaka, Zambia. They were keen to have me, but I politely asked to be allowed to make the decision after I had completed the overland trip.

After many adventures, the unlikely trio finally arrived in Bombay in mid-September, where we split up. I continued my journey by train, ferry and taxi to Sri Lanka to reach my younger brother's house, where my parents also were living. My brother, who had risen to a senior position in the Ceylon Civil Service, still a bachelor, had built the three-bedroom detached house with a government loan. 'SET' as he was called using the initials before his surname, had steadfastly refused to get married in spite of parental pressure.

My parents now turned their attention to me. Except for a couple of brief romantic encounters, in the UK, I had been purposefully single. This was the time of Mrs. Bandaranaike as the world's first woman prime minister, though economically, the country was in dire straits. There were no decent jobs for someone with my qualifications. People were praying for a chance to get out of the country. Thence, a visitor, a bachelor from the UK, was a very attractive marriage prospect. I soon met a beautiful and demure young lady, nine years my junior, speaking very good English, who was willing to share my life abroad. We had a beautiful, well-attended, traditional wedding at the bride's home, not far from Colombo, on 3rd January 1975.

I quickly telephoned the authorities in Zambia, and accepted their job offer, on condition that they recognized my changed civil status and issue me with two airplane tickets to Lusaka. They readily agreed. My new bride's parents were not exactly overjoyed when they heard that I was taking their daughter to 'darkest' Africa and not to Britain as they had hoped. I had to reassure them that eventually we would return to the 'promised land'. We flew to Lusaka in mid-January 1975 and I took up work as an occupational psychologist with the Educational and Occupational Assessment Service. Dr Jonathan Hill, a young British psychologist was the Director.

In Lusaka we were put up at a pleasant enough hotel and spent several months there in what felt like an extended honeymoon. While I spent most of my day at work, my newly acquired wife, Sue (shortened, anglicized name) remained in the hotel room. This irked her somewhat, but was soon able to secure a job as the personal secretary to an American heading the World Health Organization branch office in Lusaka. This guy and his wife, black Americans, soon became our friends, and when we finally secured a house to rent, were able to invite them for dinner. They, of course, would invite us in turn. There was a vibrant expatriate community of varied nationalities in Lusaka, and quite a few of them became our personal friends.

Then the inevitable happened, and Sue had to leave her job after eight months, to have our first baby. He arrived, a few days later than anticipated, on 21st December 1975. Not long after his first birthday, Sue was pregnant again, but the climate in Lusaka, with Ian Smith of Rhodesia bombing us whenever he felt like it, was not all that salubrious. So, reluctantly, I had to agree to let her go back to Ceylon, now Sri Lanka, all by herself, with our son T, only a few months after his first birthday, so that she could have the second baby safe in a maternity home in Colombo.

By the time I completed my 3-year contract in early 1978, our second son D, on whom I had not set my eyes, was four months old. I was in a hurry to get back, but the Zambian authorities were practically begging me to sign another contract. I had by then been promoted to one of the two Assistant Director positions of the EOAS, and for the last six months or so, was acting as Director. They wanted to confirm me as Director. I had to ignore all their pleas and return home.

However, in April 1978 when I returned to the UK alone, I was only able to find work as a clerk with a firm of West End solicitors. I found temporary accommodation of a one-bedroom flat belonging to my *alma mater*, Goldsmiths College during the summer vacation. I was therefore able to get down my family to Britain by July 1978. But our situation was far from satisfactory. When the students started arriving towards the end of September, we had to leave our flat. For the first time in our lives we were facing the prospect of homelessness.

The Royal Borough of Greenwich council put us up in temporary accommodation, a 'dump' where we were pelted with rotten eggs and our second- hand car vandalized by yobos. We stuck it out for about three months, feeding our two kids on take-away Chinese, until we were able to put down a small deposit on a terraced house in neighbouring Plumstead, in southeast London. Even with my three year stint as an occupational psychologist in Zambia, apprenticed, as it were, to experienced British psychologists, I was told that without a postgraduate qualification, I could not expect a job as a psychologist in Britain. My chances of returning to a professional work role began to look very slim indeed. When finally I was able to get my savings across to the UK from Zambia, I foolishly believed that, with a young family, leasing a corner shop selling sweets and tobacco would secure my financial future. This venture proved to be very ill-advised. It was based in New Cross not far from Goldsmiths College. The shop was broken into several times and we faced violence from putative customers who refused to pay for items they grabbed from our shelves. Even school-boys in gangs began to plague us.

My wife then took up secretarial work with a Bank in the City, and I closed the shop down to concentrate on gaining the Occupational Psychology M.Sc. degree from London University Birkbeck College. I could just about claim four years work experience in applied psychology to qualify for admission for the 2-year part time course. Just before I qualified in 1982, I was able to get a temporary job as an occupational psychologist at the Waddon Employment Rehabilitation Centre, near Croydon in Surrey. Although we could sell our house in Plumstead and move closer to my place of work in Croydon, we had great difficulty getting rid of the lease of the now empty shop premises. Finally, I managed to transfer it back to the previous owner for a pittance.

After a period of nearly a year, I was confirmed in my job with the Manpower Services Commission. I was to continue working at the Waddon Employment Rehabilitation Centre for over seven years at the same basic grade while even those new entrants to the profession whom I had helped to train were being promoted to senior positions. My manager at the ERC championed my cause since he saw me as one of the few competent psychologists he had come across during his period of service with the Manpower Services Commission. The MSC by then had undergone many changes and was renamed the Training Education and Employment Directorate. I was impelled to take my grievance of not being promoted to an Employment Tribunal. At the height of the Thatcher era this proved to be ill-advised, and I lost my case. The concept of 'institutional racism' had not yet been recognized. I was then transferred to the Manpower Services Commission Head Office in Sheffield and served one year commuting between Croydon and Sheffield spending only weekends at home. In 1989 I found myself designated a Higher Psychologist, a new designation concocted as a compromise between the Basic Grade and the Senior Grade to work at a residential Employment Rehabilitation Centre in Egham, Surrey. This involved a daily drive of over 30 miles on the motorway M20, to my place of work.

I sensed a degree of harassment in the workplace in the form of occasional missives I received from the Head Office, that I was impelled to resign in 1990. After a short period in the wilderness trying to sell insurance and the like, I took up private consultancy work as expert witness in personal injury litigation, redundancy counselling, and running job search workshops. As the work was intermittent, I wasn't making a living, and although my wife was now working for the Home Office, we failed to keep up the mortgage payments regularly. We were taken to court and nearly lost our home and all that we had worked for.

By then I had also acquired a teaching qualification from the University of Greenwich, which again proved worthless in securing employment. I was in my late fifties and no prospective employer, I realized, would take a second look at me. I had been applying for literally hundreds of jobs, even simple clerical jobs, with all my efforts proving negative. However, just in the nick of time, early in 1996, my sixtieth year, I was invited to an interview by the Royal British Legion Industries at the Royal British Legion Village, in Aylesford, Kent, a 30 mile drive away from my home. The position advertised was for an occupational psychologist, specifically for someone to start from scratch, a vocational assessment and development centre on the same lines as the state-run Employment Rehabilitation Centres. By this time the ERCs were being phased out.

I was interviewed by the Health Services Manager Mrs. Patricia Wheeler. She appeared to be impressed enough to consign a large sheaf of applications for the position lying on her table to the dustbin, and to hire me on the spot. I established from scratch the Royal British Legion Industries vocational assessment and development facility catering to the employment rehabilitation needs of ex-service men and women from all over the UK. At last, my work began to be widely appreciated and I began to contribute articles in applied psychology to professional journals. I worked at the RBLI until I reached the state retirement age of 65 in June 2001.

Until my wife retired in 2005, I tried my hand at various odd jobs like courier, and market research interviewer, but was happy to give it all up and move to Costa Blanca, Spain, in November 2005.

As a teenager, I consulted an astrologer who predicted that I would eventually become a prize-winning author. More than a decade past the biblical life span of three score years and ten, I still live with that hope.

***

A MEMORABLE VISIT

My old English teacher, Monica, now 95 years old, lives alone in Creteil, a suburb of Paris. Physically very weak, shuffling about laboriously from room to room in her fourth floor, two bedroom, rented apartment, she depends on helpers from the *Mairie* and neighbours, to keep her supplied with the essentials for daily life. She is totally *compos mentis* and uses her state and occupational pensions wisely with extreme generosity towards friends and far flung relatives. After gaining a B.A. (Hons.) in English, she began work as an English teacher in Colombo, Ceylon, but moved with her husband to London in 1960. With a post-graduate teaching qualification she had gained in London in the Fifties, she taught English at various state schools to ethnically diverse pupils in the East End until she retired in the mid-Nineties.

Even though it was her husband's terminal illness that brought her to Paris, she soon discovered a way to teach English to Parisians in a voluntary capacity. She made many friends and improved her French to a level where she now reads 'Le Monde' almost every day. After the death of her Oxford-educated husband over ten years ago, she decided to remain in the flat, communicating with her friends and relatives scattered all over the world by letter and telephone. Although she owns a personal computer, she appears not to be quite *au fait* with it, and does not use the Internet or e-mail with any consistency.

When I last spoke to her on the telephone, she kept talking about taking a two-month holiday in the south of France towards the end of the year. Whether she could accomplish this is debatable, since she has difficulty using public transport. She is a diminutive person, a shade over four feet tall, and getting in and out of a vehicle is extremely taxing for her. So, this summer, when she invited me and my wife to come over to Creteil to spend a week or so with her, I was delighted, and thought we could make an interesting and meaningful change to her daily routine. Perhaps she would reconsider plans for the end of year break. On the telephone, she was so clear and coherent in her speech, I felt that she could still be my English teacher standing in front of the class reciting 'Season of mists and mellow fruitfulness, close bosom friend of the maturing sun', more than six decades ago, at my school in Colombo. However, the pressing and immediate question was deciding on our mode of transport in travelling to Rue de Sassure, Creteil, France.

Although our friends and neighbours advised against it, my preference was to drive our small 1.2 litre car all the way to Creteil. My wife, Sue, insisted on train or plane reminding me that I am no longer the young man who once travelled overland from Cambridge to Mumbai sharing the driving with just one other person. Over ten years ago, in late autumn, I drove our RHD car from Enfield to Guardamar del Segura, stopping for two nights in France, and once in Spain. That was when we decided to settle permanently in Costa Blanca, Spain.

Except for Type 2 diabetes I had suffered over the last 20 years, controlled by daily medication, I am in reasonably good health for someone who has only a few months to reach four-score years. Under the July sun, I believed I could drive continuously for about 12 hours with short stops, and end up in a motel for the night.

The next day we planned to reach Creteil by early afternoon. Unfortunately, my Sat-Nav had packed up and I had to rely on old atlases for the trip. I also looked up Trip Advisor on Google. The route was almost entirely on toll roads and would cost us a packet. The distance from our home to Creteil was a wee bit less than 1600 km. We thought we would rest after the first 1000 km and make the next 600 km the following day, aiming to reach our destination by about midday. Sue was reluctantly, but finally convinced that we could do it.

Another consideration was the limited funds available in our joint bank account after a last minute, unexpected hefty repair bill in putting right an electrical dysfunction in the car. Although we withdrew 300 euros, this proved to be hardly sufficient for petrol, and toll charges on the Autopistas and the Autoroutes. I had to rely heavily on my credit card and the small balance left in my British bank account.

It was no easy matter climbing the Midi-Pyrenees in our Opel Corsa to get to Clermont-Ferrand by nightfall. We had done over 13 hours of driving, with my wife driving 300 km of the total 1100 km. She complained of an aching neck and I resolved not to involve her in any further driving. We did not plan to veer off the A75, but somehow ended up in a small town called Auberge, a fitting name for somewhere to spend the night. Luckily a room was available in an IBIS inn. Our lunch had been home-packed sandwiches and tea from our Thermos flask. By the time we managed to park ourselves in the motel, all the restaurants in the town were closed for the day. We managed to survive on crisps and fruit juice from the motel vending machine, until a most welcome continental breakfast the next morning.

We phoned my old teacher, Monica, and warned her that we might get late to get to her place. It would be a rather late lunch with her. Although I bought a map of Paris at a petrol station, it was not at all appropriate for negotiating the streets of the Paris suburb of Creteil. Sue had to keep ringing Monica on her mobile to ask for landmarks before we could finally get to her flat. It was about 3.00 p.m. Hunched and unsteady on her feet, Monica was standing outside her block of flats on Rue de Saussure. It was Monday 20th July and we stayed with my old teacher until Monday 27th July.

Monica had prepared for us a magnificent meal. Although Sue was not all that keen on beef, the roast was so succulent and delicious it became our main dish over the next three days. My teacher wanted to take us to a restaurant the very next day for lunch, but we demurred. My excuse was tiredness. I needed time to relax and recover. We had brought with us all the ingredients needed to make a seafood paella, except for mussels and prawns. We drove up to the nearest Carrefour to obtain these on Wednesday. There was no paella pan in the flat, so we had to resort to a shallow wok. Although at home I would have been involved in paella preparation, Sue insisted that she alone would do the job in that small kitchen. In the event, she did a magnificent job. Monica was delighted. The paella lasted over two days.

At her insistence on Friday we drove to Bois de Vincennes, losing our way more than once. Monica did not possess a map of Creteil. The neighbour from whom she could have borrowed one was away on holiday. The Paris map I had bought on the way was quite inadequate for our more local needs. Whether we had completely missed our intended destination, we never saw the forest in full bloom as Monica had described it. We roamed around for a bit and parked the car in a street full of restaurants so that we could partake of the meal which Monica insisted was to be her treat. While I kept comparing the daily menus displayed, I realised that Monica had chosen the most expensive restaurant at the end of the street, 'Le Petit Bofinger'. There was a three-course set menu for 20.90 euros including a drink. We settled for that. The *maitre'd* was very charming. While Monica and I chose salmon as the main dish, Sue chose chicken. The entree for Monica was a plate of (hard) cheese and for me it still was salmon. Sue chose a salad. The waiter brought some bread rolls too. We had a glass of white wine each. I now forget what we had for dessert.

When the bill came I expected it to be slightly under 65 euros. Monica didn't want me to see the *'l'addition'*. After she paid with her Visa bank card, I saw that it was over 109 euros. It was not three times 20.90 euros plus service charge as I had surmised, but each item individually priced including the bread rolls. According to Monica, there was no point making a fuss at that point, she took it all in her stride. It was not an easy task to find our way home from Bois de Vincennes without a local map or a Sat-Nav. After many unnecessary and tiresome diversions we finally made it by late afternoon.

Some of our friends had hinted at the dangers to holiday travellers from highway robbers and bogus cops. Thankfully, we did not encounter such horrors on our journey. Occasionally there were those who did not like our overtaking them and made it a point to aggressively overtake us in turn. That didn't bother me. On the Autoroutes there were lorries overtaking slower ones and forcing us to the third lane needing to exceed the 130 kph speed limit. Few kept to this speed limit anyway, and for the first time, to my amazement, our four-year old car too exceeded 160 kph on some stretches. However, the Midi-Pyrenees was a challenge, where we were often forced on to the extra slow lane on the extreme right, and crawl on first gear. Later, to my distress, I discovered that I had been caught speeding twice, and had to fork out 90 euros in fines plus the bank charges. No more distant driving, admonished Sue.

The highlight of our stay with my old teacher was the visit to the Asian trading quarter in Paris. Knowing my limitations in finding my way around by car, Monica suggested that we travel to La Chapelle by taxi. Less stress for Sue, and we agreed. I forget which day of the week it was, but the taxi took about half-an-hour. We were shopping for traditional Asian, in this case, Sri Lankan Tamil-imported foodstuffs. Monica said that what she bought there, would last her for the next six months. Sue also bought Sri Lankan vegetables and herbs rarely seen in Spain. Hailing a return taxi was no easy matter. Finally, after a short walk to a taxi rank, we found someone willing to take us to Creteil. He explained to us that taxi-drivers were not allowed to take up fares on the return journey from the suburbs. Therefore, they preferred to ply their trade mainly within the precincts of Paris. The taxi fare for the shopping expedition totalled just over 100 euros.

We decided to make our return journey on Monday 27th using the national routes avoiding Autoroutes, at least within France. We started inauspiciously at 7.30 a.m. not being able to get out of Creteil, going round and round for over an hour. Finally, when we found the road to Orleans we realised that the numbers prefixed with N given on our old atlas had changed. That was only a minor distraction, but the diversions and road works on the national roads were so extensive that we lost our way many times adding hours to the return journey. Just before dark, after only 590 km we got to a place called Issoire about 20 km south of Clermont-Ferrand. We managed to get a room for the night in the centre of this small town for 66 euros, a little more than what we paid at IBIS, but much more comfortable.

On the 28th at 8.30 a.m. we took the French Autoroute A71, crossed over to Spain and followed the Spanish AP7/E15 to the roundabout at Junction 745 to get us to Lo Crispin, our urbanization. It was about 9.00 p.m. by the time we got home in fading daylight, having done just over a 3500 km, round trip.

Sight-seeing in Paris is no longer a priority for me, but Sue kept complaining that she was denied the pleasure of bumping into Mona Lisa at the Louvre. As for me, until the end of my days, I shall treasure the memory of the few precious moments I spent, reminiscing with my former teacher.

***

A WRITER'S GIFT

'I don't have to go inside his flat mum', was Jenny's response when Rosie cautioned her daughter about the stranger who had recently moved into the flat next-door. Rosie, her husband Harry, and their daughter Jennifer lived at No. 1, a two-bed ground floor council flat on the Whitfield Estate. Rosie settled down to being a full-time mum almost immediately after she married Harry, although she had worked as a barmaid during their courtship. Harry worked with a building firm as a general labourer. They considered themselves lucky to have managed to rent a council flat just before Jenny was born. Their new neighbour at No. 3, empty for almost a year, was a middle-aged single man who had moved in only recently.

Harry Sutphen often worked overtime and felt there was no need for Rosie to go out and work even part-time to supplement the household income. Rosie, on her part, was quite happy to be the stay-at-home mum. She had enough on her hands cooking, cleaning, washing, ironing, occasionally sewing, and looking after the house. Jenny needed less attention once she started attending the local Comprehensive. Her bedroom was full of books by authors like Enid Blyton and Roald Dahl. From the time, she started attending primary school, Harry provided her with weekly pocket money, of which she saved some in a piggy bank, and most of the rest spent on buying books.

Once a week, Harry would spend the evening with his mates at the local Bard's Head pub and Jenny would visit her mother Doreen who lived with her unmarried sister Sandra, a short bus ride away. Harry cycled to work daily two miles to the head office of his employer Benson & Sons plc. He would be taken with other employees to various building sites by company transport and brought back to the head office at the end of the working day.

Harry and Rosie, not being car owners, when feeling the need for a break, would book a coach tour to Southend, Brighton or Blackpool. Alton Towers was a favourite venue of theirs. Jenny increasingly began to enjoy these trips, and last year wrote an account of Alton Towers to read out in class. Harry and Rosie had never been interested in foreign travel. However, when Jenny started learning French, on one occasion, they managed a Eurostar day trip across the English Channel. Jenny also started learning computing at school. Harry put in extra hours to earn enough to buy Jenny a laptop and a printer. Jenny spent many hours in her room doing homework using the laptop.

Next door to the Sutphens at number 3 lived an old couple who had bought the leasehold of the flat from the council sometime in the past. Tragically, about a year ago, the couple died in a car accident. There were legal problems about inherited ownership, which took a long time to resolve. Now at last there was an occupant, a spritely, middle-aged man who had bought the leasehold property. This was Don Withen, a well-known writer, who was said to be suffering from an incurable terminal disease, and had decided to end his days alone in obscurity. Number 3 Whitfield Estate suited him fine. Don reassured the neighbours that his illness was a genetic condition and not contagious, but politely refused invitations to visit them or to invite them in turn.

Don Withen did not have visitors at all, except for regular visits by a doctor and nurse from the local hospital. All his meals, except breakfast, were either delivered as takeaways or, he would take a taxi to any one of the restaurants he fancied in the locality. He made regular trips to his bank or his lawyers by taxi. Once a fortnight Sally, a domestic cleaner would come to tidy up the flat. She had her own key to the flat.

Although Don Withen chose isolation, something about Jenny appeared to have attracted his attention. One day he intercepted Jenny when she was returning home from school and asked her whether she was willing to help him.

'You know I won't invite people into my flat,' he said.

'Yeah, but what can I do for you? Jenny responded cautiously.

'I'll pay for your help. All you have to do is type out what I give you - handwritten pages - and load it into a memory stick. Once finished, you hand it back to me.'

'Oh well, I can do that. No problem,' answered Jenny. She was flattered Don Withen had sussed out that she was handy with a computer.

'Okay, I'll hand you the script next time I see you. Bye for now.'

'Bye.'

Once or twice a week, Don would stop Jenny on her way back from school and hand her a few sheets of handwritten notes along with a memory stick. The handwriting was clear enough for Jenny to be able to type out the manuscript on the laptop and load it on to the memory stick. She always looked up the dictionary if there were words she did not understand. She used the spell-checker often. It did not worry her that she did not comprehend much of what she transcribed. When she had completed the job, she would ring the doorbell at number 3 and hand over the memory stick and notes to Mr Withen. Jenny's work contained around four to five pages of Don's manuscripts most days, and she always received cash at the rate of £1.00 per page from him.

Very soon Jenny's work for Ian earned her about ten pounds a week. The piggy bank was no longer appropriate to stash away her savings, so Harry opened a savings account for her at the Post Office.

'All this will come in handy when you get to university, Jen.'

Obviously Harry had high hopes for his daughter's future. Rosie too was elated at her daughter's capacity to earn money at such a young age.

Then, out of the blue, disaster struck. Harry's earnings had been dwindling due to lack of overtime. Suddenly he was laid off, and was forced to claim unemployment benefit. Now Jenny chose to give all her earnings to Rosie for everyday expenses, mitigating their hardship somewhat. Don appeared to have sensed their plight and often handed Jenny a bit more than the agreed sum.

While Harry was out signing on at the Job Centre, Rosie made her way to the Bard's Head pub, a place she had not been in for years. She bought herself a half pint of lager and started chatting with some of her old friends. The present landlady, daughter of the couple who owned the pub, recognised Rosie and knew her situation. She offered Rosie part-time work, two evenings a week. Rosie accepted gratefully and began work the very next day.

Harry was required to attend job clubs and listen to talks on how to present himself at job interviews. He even prepared a CV with the help of an adviser. Months passed, but there was no sign that Harry would ever find a job. Harry was at times forced to resort to a food bank to supplement the weekly purchase of groceries. Rosie encouraged him to keep up with his former work mates at the Bard's Head pub by handing him a few quid from her earnings.

To make matters worse that autumn, Don became seriously ill and was confined to bed. Jenny's source of income ceased abruptly. One day, after a visit from the doctor and nurse, he was rushed to hospital by ambulance. Within a few days he was dead. According to the local weekly newspaper, Don Withen, the well-known writer, was cremated without ceremony or publicity, strictly in keeping with his wishes. His estate was divided among various charities, foremost, for medical research to prevent genetic transmission of the illness which killed him. His flat reverted to ownership of the local council. A local firm of solicitors dealing with Don Withen's will and testament, Messrs. Pritchard and Johnson were responsible for dealing with the beneficiaries.

Two weeks later, a registered letter from Messrs. Pritchard and Johnson arrived at number 1 Whitfield Estate. The Sutphen family was invited to a meeting with the law firm. Harry telephoned the solicitors and agreed to meet them the very next day. They were able to glean from the solicitors that it had something to do with Don Withens' will.

The outcome was that all Sutphens' financial troubles were over. Jenny would receive £1000 a month from Don Withen's estate until she reached eighteen. She would then be the beneficiary of a trust fund which would enable her to attend a university anywhere in the Western world, all fees, travel and living expenses paid for. She was also the recipient of royalties from Don Withen's latest book, a collection of essays entitled 'A Writer's Gift'.

When she obtained a copy, Jenny was pleasantly surprised and elated that it was dedicated to: 'Jennifer Sutphen, my helpful neighbour'.

***

BOUNDEN DUTY

Nina and I were lounging under the brightly striped sun shade on the terrace of our retirement home in Pinar del Mar, Costa Deliciosa. We were both in our T-shirts, shorts and slippers, although it was still early spring. The summer was already promising to be a scorcher.

I have this theory that as married couples get older they begin to resemble each other more, and that is reflected in their mannerisms and even in the way they dress. Nina and I both discovered reduced demands on our time and energy, since moving to Spain. Did we have nothing more pressing to talk about than our daily chores?

Nina put the glossy magazine she was leafing through on the rest of the pile of reading material spread out on the floor. Many of them were leaflets produced weekly by local supermarkets. We had both been working hard to earn a living, but now there was nothing more to strive for, since we were entitled to our four-weekly state pensions paid regularly into our joint account at a local bank. We were here to enjoy a quiet life. Our family obligations over with kids grown up, having sold our house in the UK, settled all bills, we felt free to go our own way.

'But of course we'll still have a job on our hands - especially when they all start dropping in on us to see how we are coping with all this sunshine, sea, and sangria in Spain'.

'In the meantime, don't forget, we have to do our shopping, marketing and keeping the house clean and the garden tidy. You know, I use the washing machine at least three times a week' Nina was reminding me that she was still the housewife.

:You may sit around doing the crossword all day, but I have work to do'.

'Don't be like that! You know I help. I do all the washing up, and help with the cooking, cutting up the meat, vegetables – and, you didn't complain when I won the cryptic crossword in the local newspaper and took you out for a meal'.

'We should get out more, I think'.

'Besides, I am the one who drives you around'.

'Yea, but I should be doing a lot more driving, in case...'

'What d'ya mean; in case I pop off?'

'Don't be silly. You know what I mean'.

'Yes of course – you mean when I get drunk on a night out'.

'Be serious for a minute will you... When we start our Spanish classes next month, we could take turns driving to and from the 'ayuntamiento'.

'Okay. You drive to, and I'll drive from. That way you'll learn to find a parking space and improve your reversing skills'.

Just then, I noticed an elderly couple standing by our front gate.

Bill and Wendy from two doors up the street was also a retired couple settling down to a life in the sun. Roughly our age, perhaps the only thing that was different about them was that they owned a cat which was their pride and joy. It was their boast that Fluffy cost them a small fortune to bring over to Costa Deliciosa.

They were now about to pass our front gate carrying a black bag each, full of their domestic rubbish, which most certainly included the cat litter. They would dump these on the local authority provided bin at the end of the street. We too followed this ritual, repeated almost every day. In the UK, while even weekly clearances were uncertain, the rubbish bins on every street in our urbanization were emptied nightly by the local council.

'We are going to Trish's for fish and chips in a minute. Care to join us? 'Bill ventured as he stopped by the gate and lowered his rubbish bag. Wendy could not resist trying to smell the hibiscus flowers leaning over the parapet, although I was sure she knew hibiscus was odourless.

'OK..., in our car, seeing it's parked just outside'.

Although we had adequate parking space in our front garden, I preferred to leave the car outside during much of the day.

'No..oo problema'.

That was probably as much Spanish as Bill could muster, except of course 'Hola' and Buenos dias' that you just could not avoid hearing when encountering the locals. Bill and Wendy took every opportunity to patronize the restaurants run by compatriots, and fish and chips were one of their staples. They also assiduously shopped for lamb and beef at the local supermarkets for their Sunday roast. Nina and I had a different approach to our culinary requirements and tried to adjust to the locally available Mediterranean cuisine. We experimented with paella and grilled sardines and ate more shell–fish and chicken eschewing red meat, which we explained to ourselves as a health precaution. On the few occasions we were able to persuade Bill and Wendy to accompany us to a Spanish restaurant, even if they tried paella as the first course, they were happier with liver, or lamb chops and chips, as the main course.

While Bill and Wendy returned from their 'rubbish walk' and changed into more colourful costumes including the mandatory straw hats, Nina and I put on our sandals and the rather mundane cloth caps, before we were ready for the ten minute drive to Trish's Café.

Driving to town was no sweat. There were hardly any traffic lights. Instead, there were huge roundabouts which were without exception all beautifully landscaped. The broad, dual carriageway with clearly marked lanes was a newly built modern alternative to an old, abandoned, single- lane country road still visible alongside the Autopista. Wendy noticed from a distance that there were depressions on this lane at marked intervals and asked me whether they took the role of sleeping policemen.

The service road ('camino') from our urbanization to the main roundabout had three humps (sleeping policemen) laid at about 50-yard intervals. Earlier, Wendy had complained that I drove too fast over these humps for her comfort.

'Since they are not humps but dips in the lane, they've got to be sleeping policewomen'.

I thought I was being funny, but this started off a discussion between Wendy and Nina on the appalling state of equal opportunities in Spain. In all legal matters the male took precedence, they both averred. We had a duty to change the status quo. What is the point of being part of the European Union if equal opportunity concerns did not apply across the Union?

I reflected on the fact that the ancient Chinese were wont to place highly stylized lions at the entrances to their stately buildings. They totally ignored the female of the species. I wasn't quite sure how the ancient Egyptians treated this gender imbalance, but I was pretty sure that this bias was common to all nations and cultures.

What I now saw to the left of me confirmed my hypothesis. There were statues of two male lions, rampant, on either side of a large double iron gate at the entrance to an imposing mansion. Why only male lions with their flowing manes, why not lionesses without such ostentation but with equal rights to be recognized? They had as much right to be ornamental as the ubiquitous male. I could detect only a backhanded compliment in the adage that 'the female of the species is deadlier than the male'. I put these arguments to Wendy and Nina who both went very quiet for a while before agreeing.

'Yes, we must do something about it'.

I concluded that they saw it as their bounden duty.

We enjoyed our fish and chips without further discussion on equal opportunities or much of anything else. Then we took an exhilarating walk down the sandy beach along Costa Deliciosa before returning home to Pinar del Mar.

***

WORK ETHIC

Alan drove thirty miles out of town to get to work. The workplace, a Rehabilitation Centre, where Alan was a therapist, sprawled across a 60-acre plot with a period mansion as its centrepiece. Outlying buildings were new, one-storey, low-slung and brick-built with pine wood cladding, possibly emulating a modern Scandinavian style.

He drove uphill on the secondary road passing a wooded stretch with no buildings in sight. Occasionally through the thick trunks of tall trees he would glimpse meadows and fields with clusters of farm animals forming brown and black patches on the otherwise unrelieved green. Mercifully, the devastation wrought on the flora and fauna of southern England by two recent hurricanes had spared the worst for this part of the country.

Although he was too busy or too lazy these days to take a stroll around the grounds of the Centre, he knew that he would have heard if anything had been amiss. All those magnificent trees he could see from his office window were still intact. He always said that he was happier on days when he could see more magpies than aeroplanes in the sky looking out of his window. He warmed to the hare that ran across his path as he climbed the sloping drive which led to the car park with space reserved for him alongside other staff. Alan's name painted by a client from the Woodwork Section on a plank signified his reserved parking slot.

With a steaming mug of coffee in his hand, Alan wandered into the Instructors' common room. It was his turn to brief the Instructors on the week's intake of clients, or rehabilitees, as they were designated. The Instructors were invariably grey-haired, ageing gentlemen except for the Commercial Section Instructor, who was an attractive young blonde. She instructed and assessed clients with clerical and secretarial work aspirations. The majority of her clients were women. Sister Joan from the medical centre was the only other female present at the briefing. She was able to fill them in on the various disabilities that the clients presented, psychiatric disabilities providing the most discussion and often dismay as to what could be achieved in attempting to rehabilitate them. The Instructors all had their specialisations, like bench engineering, carpentry/joinery, and electrical engineering. During absences due to leave or sickness the instructors had no difficulty covering for each other. They always boasted that they had more than one string to their bows, hinting in contrast, that a therapist like Alan had only a limited range of skills that, to them, hardly detectable.

Alan used a short stretch of the busy orbital motorway before he got to the secondary road, which often provided occasions for him to muse on his vulnerability, if he became disabled himself. A road traffic accident could result in him being injured and disabled, possibly for life. After a spell in hospital, he thought, he would be asked to volunteer for a course at the Rehabilitation Centre. They would assess him for the type of work he could now do for a living. He may have to live on state benefits and probably have to be bussed from the nearest railway station, as he would no longer be able to, or, allowed to, drive. He remembered how a client had objected to being identified as a disabled person and having to travel in a bus so designated. The thinking behind painting the bus with the Rehabilitation Centre logo in bold letters was that it was considered helpful to the partially sighted and the mentally retarded. So long as there was a stigma attached to disability, a reluctance to be labelled was understandable, Alan concluded.

"Where would you put me if I came to you disabled", he asked the Chief Instructor who had just walked into the Common Room.

"What makes you think you are so very able now", quipped the Chief. "In fact, only the other day, the doctor said that if he wanted a quiet little job when he retired, he would seriously consider applying for yours".

"I believe I can give you a few good years, but I'll still take you on. C'mon outside", Alan motioned towards the door without the slightest intention of being taken at his word. Indeed, he was much younger than the Chief Instructor.

Alan liked to be thought of as one of the lads. Although not required to do so, he insisted on using the instructors' Common Room to sit and drink his daily mug of morning coffee. He shared other official breaks with his professional colleagues like the nursing sister, the remedial gymnast and the social worker, in the Restaurant, which in an earlier day would have been called the canteen. Geoff, the centre manager would join the professional clique during coffee-breaks. They had their own table to which they gravitated although nobody had designated it as such. The staff and clients were separated at these times, the restaurant being bisected by a partition for this purpose. Newspaper accounts and press photographs of a past royal visit to the premises adorned the internal walls of the restaurant on the clients' side. The staff side walls were bare except for an illuminated board declaring the day's menu.

The client suffering from multiple sclerosis was a hauntingly beautiful young woman. She had come to be assessed for redeployment by her employer in a less demanding capacity, possibly as a part-time receptionist. Alternatively, with new technology, she could be one of those people, who could be retrained to work from home. However, the Rehabilitation Centre did not quite reflect the changing patterns of employment or occupations outside. A few traditional trades like market gardening, machine setting and operating, carpentry and electrical installation were represented, but a large segment of service provision like catering or marketing and sales, were only indirectly addressed, if at all.

Alan's good intentions were constantly being undermined by those clients who thought of themselves as poets, writers, actors, and artists, with the odd musician thrown in. They felt they were under pressure to adapt to uncongenial industrial and commercial work to reduce government unemployment statistics and save on benefit handouts.

"Be realistic", Alan would tell them at interview, how many of us can earn a living writing poetry or painting pictures? As regards the performing arts …" he would roll his eyes heavenwards indicating no wish to discuss the matter any further.

There were those who came to the Centre with the fixed idea that the only saviour in the employment wilderness was the computer. Whatever their background and facility with English and maths was, they seemed to think that if only they were given the chance to sit in front of a PC, they would not fail to land that well-paid job. Nevertheless, only a very small proportion of the total client group would proceed to either appropriate training and further education, or suitable and adequately paid jobs. Some were recommended Sheltered Work or attendance at a Day Centre, while quite a few others remained forever 'looking for work'. Still others, the 'recycled' clients, according to Alan, kept returning to the Rehabilitation Centre after brief unsatisfactory episodes of work ending in absenteeism and often dismissal.

What made Alan take up this relatively low paid, low status job as a rehabilitation therapist? Earlier he had pursued a well-paid career in private industry that he eventually began to loathe as hypocritical and exploitative. He had thought that the state-funded Centre did useful work that no other agency was equipped to do. Now, he was not so sure. There was talk of cutbacks and a freeze on recruitment of staff. Support staff in the guise of clerks and typists appeared and disappeared with alarming rapidity. Long serving trade instructors availed themselves of early voluntary retirement.

It was sadly ironical that an agency dedicated to the task of directing disabled and disadvantaged persons towards productive employment had staff unsure of their own future job prospects. One rumour was that the Centre was to be privatized. The site could be worth a few million pounds sterling. Perhaps a leisure park would be built. A property developer could make a fortune building three or four executive houses on the site. Another rumour was that a more powerful Ministry had its beady eye on the premises. Impersonal memoranda from the head office gave assurances that nothing drastic would be undertaken without full and proper consultation.

Alan reported back on the clients to referring agencies after collecting information of ratings on work samples from the trade instructors. Medical information, social worker's observations and the remedial gymnast's interventions were also available for Alan to come to conclusions regarding recommendations for a client's future re-training or work role.

Alan looked out of the window admiring the ground cover plants outside. The green of the low-growing bushes were broken by the taller flowering plants spaced about four or five feet apart. There was an indoor plant on Alan's side-table placed against the window, a geranium with a single flower in a small brown plastic pot. Alan kept most of his working documents –mimeographed forms in various colours – in a glass fronted cabinet placed against the wall in front of his table. Two high backed metal frame chairs for his clients and a hat/coat stand, completed the furniture inventory in his room. Alan's name followed by his degree qualifications printed on a card was stuck on the door outside at eye-level.

"I came here just to give my wife a break … sitting at home all day … getting under her feet … No good for a marriage, is it?" drawled the fifty-year old former lorry driver wriggling in the chair opposite Alan. Alan merely nodded and looked at the man with, what he thought, was sympathetic concern.

"Can't sit still longer than a minute. Can't stand either. Need to walk around to ease this blooming back pain." The man got up indicating a need to pace up and down. Alan made what he thought were encouraging noises.

"My doctor says that I am finished as far as work is concerned, but the Social Security bloke insists that I can do something. When I go for job interviews and they hear about my back, nobody 'effing' wants to know."

"You have fifteen more years to go before the state retirement age", said Alan evenly.

"… and I am bloody well not happy about living on handouts either."

"Is there a case for claiming compensation for your injuries?"

The man fell silent for a moment or two. "Not banking on that", he said in a reflective tone. "All in the hands of solicitors."

"So I see… Has the other party admitted liability?"

"Oh yes. They are haggling over the figures now. May still go to court."

The man, who had been twisting around while pacing the room, straightened up and sat down in one of the chairs with a sigh.

"Right. We'll give you some tests … Nothing very difficult. Do the best you can. No point killing yourself. If you are in the slightest pain, stop and tell the instructor. Is that ok?"

"Fair enough. I'll give it a go." The man got up to leave, then bent over to face Alan. "You'll give me a piece of paper saying I am not fit for work, won't you?"

"We'll say as objectively as we can what you can and cannot do based on our tests and work samples over the next couple of weeks you are with us. Would that be a help to you?" Alan stuck to his formula.

"Suppose so … keep the benefit people off my back for a while."

"Don't expect the report for a few weeks though … We don't have a typist at the moment. Staff cuts y'know."

"Oh! I'll keep myself busy fishing," the man grinned as he disappeared down the corridor.

Alan was not planning for retirement or redundancy when he hadn't even reached middle age. He dismissed thoughts of becoming disabled that he had entertained earlier. Alan put the file he was scribbling on aside and started calculating how long he would have to work before he could earn his permanent holiday in the sun. He wasn't thinking of fishing exactly, but the sun, sea and sand of the Mediterranean featured strongly in his calculations. In the meantime, he had a job convincing his many and diverse clients of the value of subscribing to the work ethic.

***

MY FRIEND THE LIBRARIAN

In my reclusive life, libraries have been an important feature. Starting with school libraries at my primary school and later at secondary school, I went on to have access to the London University Library as a mature student. As an itinerant, I was, successively, a member of each public library in Greater London local authority areas I happened to live. Finally after graduating, I had the good fortune of becoming a member of the truly incomparable British Library now housed in a splendid edifice in St Pancras.

Moving away from the rarefied and impersonal world of public libraries, I want to talk about a school friend who later became a librarian, a fully qualified chartered librarian. He won a Commonwealth Scholarship to study librarianship at the University of Nottingham in the early Sixties. He wasn't actually a friend but an acquaintance at the time, as he was two classes ahead of me at secondary school in Colombo, Ceylon. I remember him as the leader of the school debating team, speaking eloquently at inter-school debating contests, on whatever happened to be the allocated topic. On such occasions he would dress up in a shiny white satin drill suit which set off to good effect the flashy striped school tie in maroon and gold.

Since there were no restrictions on Commonwealth citizens taking up residence in Britain at the time, Suresh decided to stay on after he qualified. That was the time when I became his friend, having renewed my acquaintance with him as a newly arrived Commonwealth immigrant myself, desperately in search of familiar faces to combat social isolation. Unlike my learned friend, who had already spent a couple of years under the tutelage of the renowned poet Philip Larkin at a prestigious public library in the north of the country, I, with only a secondary school-leaving certificate to my name, was forced to take on whatever unskilled jobs I could find.

Trying hard to better myself, I eventually gained a Bachelor of Arts degree from the University of London. With only a Lower Second, I never advanced in the employment stakes above the rank of clerical assistant or administrative assistant in large establishments hiring hundreds of employees at a time. As boredom set in, I tried job-switching for a while but soon found that I no longer continued to have the skills nor the background that employers demanded with every fresh job interview I attended. Finally, I found a job driving a delivery van which gave me the freedom and variety during my working day. It afforded me the space to dream, and retain some iota of self-esteem, without being the subject of constant put downs by fellow office wage slaves earning a pittance.

In the meantime, my friend the librarian too appeared to stagnate in the lowest rung in his career. He fought verbally with colleagues and superiors arguing that he never got the recognition he deserved. He kept applying for more senior positions with better pay, but was always turned down. He complained bitterly of prejudice and maintained that colleagues less qualified and experienced than him received preference due to uncontestable but utterly irrelevant similarities between them and their bosses. Suresh ended up always as the odd man out.

To be frank, I personally doubted whether Suresh made any attempt to fit in with the British way of life. He had a very good command of the English language and, if you take my word for it, spoke without any discernible awkwardness in accent. However, he professed to be a total vegetarian and an uncompromising teetotaler. He would never go into a pub or bar with his colleagues and did not attend their parties or celebrations. It is difficult to imagine him being at ease at librarians' annual gatherings or conferences, which I am sure he must have been required to attend as part of his training and professional development.

At the time, Suresh was renting a bachelor pad in Camden Town not too far from his place of work at the British Library, then located on the same premises as the British Museum. For him, it was a very convenient place to be living in, due to the many Indian vegetarian restaurants close by. Suresh was a fan of the late Krishnamurthy, and persuaded me to attend lectures given by the great man at Brockwood

Park in Hampshire. Much as I would have liked it, I was never able to understand fully, let alone act upon the wise counsel, that Krishnamurthy so obviously offered to the many thousands of his followers.

Suddenly, without warning, Suresh left his rented one-bedroom flat and disappeared. He had been thoroughly disillusioned and disappointed at his lack of progress within the profession, in contrast to my situation which I had fatalistically accepted as my lot in life. In our late thirties we were both single men without the slightest prospect of our civil status changing in the foreseeable future. We saw ourselves as condemned to be 'losers' in our different ways, although Suresh appeared to take his situation much more seriously and was unremitting in his search for a solution.

After a long silence, Suresh did finally contact me. He had taken up a job in Adelaide, Australia, paying him more than treble what he had earned in London. So, he had made the break and was now enjoying his just rewards. What was even more interesting was that he had married a Swiss girl, someone he met at one of the Krishnamurthy gatherings in Saanen, Switzerland. It was a matter of pride for him that Theresa was almost two decades his junior. Suresh was at pains to point out that it was a Platonic relationship and that the marriage was more a spiritual union rather than a carnal coupling. In plain terms, as I understood it, the marriage was never consummated and would remain so forever.

I was very surprised at this development as the bachelor Suresh used to frequent strip clubs and other shady joints in Soho in the Sixties, and on one memorable occasion even persuaded me to sample the delights offered there. He also owned a dozen or so pornographic prints which he assured me were copies of a very small fraction of what was to be found in a collection not open to the public in one of the academic libraries he had worked. Perhaps he had disposed of them before he got married. Or, were the couple given to poring over them, and although aroused, given to swearing eternal abstinence to each other? Obviously Suresh had moved on, literally and metaphorically.

The next I heard of Suresh was that he had hurt his back carrying large tomes of the Australian version of the British Hansard, proceedings of the Australian House of Representatives.

He was promptly pensioned off and was paid a handsome lump as severance pay.

Once freed from his onerous duties, Suresh had taken the opportunity to travel to India with his unsullied bride, and ended up in an ashram run for the followers of Sai Baba, said to be a living incarnation of the Hindu god Krishna. There, Suresh and his wife had completely imbibed the Hindu traditions of simple living and renunciation of worldly ambitions. However, this did not stop them eventually from moving to the south of France and building their own home on a plot of land purchased a few miles inland from the international tourist haven of Nice.

When I finally got to visit them in a hired car (neither of them drove, or owned a car), I found them both very content and hospitable, living in a spacious, detached, three-bedroom, brand new house with a large high-walled garden. Theresa proudly declared that she had a hand in its design. I was to spend a whole week with them. Their gastronomic preferences, as was to be expected, were entirely vegetarian. They grew most of their vegetables. It was Suresh who prepared the daily breakfast of nuts and yoghurt. Theresa would prepare both lunch and dinner of vegetarian lasagna and similar delicacies. I felt that the presence of a guest was the only reason they went to the trouble of preparing three meals a day. These preparations were all entirely edible and even quite tasty. They regularly drank Soya milk and freshly squeezed fruit juice. Surprisingly, I did not miss my occasional glass of wine or the more frequent pint of bitter. I repaid their hospitality by driving them to the seaside and one or two places of interest in Provence. We never entered a bar or restaurant on these occasions. We had what we needed, all vegetarian, brought with us, complete in a picnic basket.

The entire first floor of the house, except for the hallway, where the couple had separate sleeping arrangements laid out on the floor, was given over to the Library. True to his vocation, Suresh had lined up scores of shelves with his life-long accumulation of books arranged in alphabetical order by author name, and classified according to the time-honored Dewey Decimal Classification System. The Library, needless to say, was Suresh's pride and joy. Oh, I forgot to mention that Suresh had written many books on a range of religious and spiritual subjects which were invariably published at his own expense by an Indian publisher. I did own a few copies of these that Suresh had presented me at some time or other in the past, although I had not found them of much interest to me, and therefore had neglected to read. All this output now lined one of the shelves of his library. There were also cardboard boxes full of them on the floor perhaps awaiting distribution, I knew not where.

On the last evening of my visit with my friend, we discussed our school days and even spoke a few words in our now rather rusty mother tongue. Early next morning, it was just when I was putting my case in the back seat of the rented car that he owned up to the practice of drinking his own urine first thing in the morning. Theresa too admitted to having been persuaded to share this ritual. I had once read somewhere that an Indian President or Prime Minister had indulged himself in this practice while publicly extolling its healing properties. Although I was not shocked, I felt a certain repugnance towards their, evidently harmless, eccentricity.

Nevertheless, the one thing I wished to remember from my unlikely-to-be repeated visit was Suresh's fervently expressed desire to leave in his will the entire contents of his home library to the British Library in London. Driving alone back to my dreary London pad across the vast expanse that is France, I wondered how the British Library would respond to this gesture of magnanimity on the part of my librarian friend Suresh, once he was no more.

PARKING TICKET

It took me a while to get used to driving our newly acquired left-hand-drive car on the right hand side of the road. My wife Sue and I had just moved to Costa Blanca, Spain, from the UK. The Costas of Spain are not only the Brits' favourite holiday destination; they have also made it a place for a permanent abode, and many like us, a place to spend their retirement years in the sun.

The Mediterranean was not the only reason we drove almost daily to the nearest coastal town. Indeed during the winter months there had to be other diversions away from just sun, sea and sand. We liked eating out, visiting the theatre and concert halls, and watching street celebrations and fiestas. However, there being no public transport system operating between our urbanization and the town, like most others, we were constrained to use the car for all our journeys, whether locally, or further afield. The only bugbear in all this was the extreme difficulty of finding a parking space in our busy coastal town of Torrevieja with its narrow streets and limited spaces allocated for street parking.

Every time I managed to find the rare spot between two cars Sue expressed great uneasiness over my struggles to get our car reversed into the slot. To be honest, I was not all that comfortable in such manoeuvres and often had to abandon the attempt and move elsewhere. However, as I discovered soon enough, even with only a few municipal public car parks in town, two or three of them underground, we could always manage to find an unoccupied space in one of them. Even so, my preference was always to park on the side of a street, if there was a free space between parked cars, rather than in a town's car park. This was not because I was stingy and did not want to pay the parking charges, but because I found the pre-and post-parking operations extremely tedious. Pressing the right button to obtain the ticket and sticking it in the right slot on departure, finding the right coins while a queue was forming behind us – all of that - tested me to the limit. Old age – I suppose!

Sue kept insisting that the car was much safer underground than leaving it exposed on the street. She had a point, because cars had been broken into, and damaged by vandals or by careless, inexperienced drivers. My objections however, stemmed from an occasion in the past where my inability to hang on to the parking ticket obtained from the automatic dispenser until time of payment, caused a great deal of frustration, panic, and time-wasting, before we were able to get away.

My difficulties arose mainly from the fact that I hardly ever carried a wallet with me. Heeding advice given about pickpockets and aggressive beggars, I had decided to carry just enough loose cash in my trouser-pocket to meet the needs of the day. During the summer I wore shorts, a tee shirt and a pair of sandals, but in winter, I opted for a long sleeved shirt, a pair of long trousers or jeans and a pullover or jumper. Of course I dispensed with the sandals and took to wearing shoes or trainers in winter. Whatever the outfit, I only had my trouser pockets to carry personal belongings like car/house keys, a hanky and some cash. It seemed obvious that there was no way I could keep a flimsy piece of paper like a parking ticket safe on my person.

This is where Sue came to the rescue. She always carried her handbag but on my advice kept cash to a minimum. Since the incident of the lost ticket, every time we parked underground, the parking ticket was secure inside her handbag.

On an unusually cold day in April, the day we went to see the Racquel Peña dance troupe at the Teatro Municipal in town, we parked the car at the Cultural Centre underground car park.

After the performance we rushed to our car. But where was the parking ticket? While everybody else was moving away, we were stuck in the underground car park with Sue desperately rummaging in her handbag for the parking ticket. She suddenly turned towards me insisting that she never had it in the first place.

'But you always have it with you.'

'Not this time. I think you got it. Don't you remember?'

'Look carefully. It must be there in your handbag.'

Sue was furious. She shot out of her seat and emptied the entire contents of her handbag on to the seat. No sign of the ticket anywhere.

It took us a lot time and also some extra cash before we were finally able to get out of that car park.

Of course, it struck me like a bolt as soon as we got home, well past midnight.

Unusually for me that day I was wearing a parka over my pullover. We had been to Zenia Boulevard, the brand new shopping centre, that morning, where for the first time, I became the proud owner of an anorak. And there it was, safely tucked inside the top left-hand pocket of my newly acquired fashionable item of clothing, the elusive parking ticket. My apologies to Sue were profuse, but she was not very conciliatory.

'Now you know where to stick your parking ticket, don't bother me again!'

***

THE LAST SPACE TOURIST

Yesterday, 12th November 2046, all communication between the International Space Station III and NASA came to an abrupt stop. The planet earth had ceased to function. Intense radiation on the earth's surface had made it now completely uninhabitable by any sentient species. I, along with the two Chinese astronauts who manned the space shuttle that brought me here, witnessed the nuclear conflagrations which initiated the total destruction of the planet earth. From where I am sitting, I can glimpse the holocaust still rampaging across what used to be the main metropolitan centers and capital cities of the advanced industrial nations on earth. All communication between the space station and earth ceased precisely at 1508 hours SSMT yesterday.

For centuries, there have been unresolved tensions between various political, ethnic, national, and religious groupings in the world. However, that it would come to an all-out nuclear war at the time it happened, exactly on 12th November 2046, could not have been predicted even by a present-day Nostradamus. In addition to terrorist organizations like Al Qaeda and ISIS or Daesh, states like Iran, Iraq, Afghanistan, Syria and various African fundamentalist Muslim states had been aligned against, the USA, UK, Australia, New Zealand, Israel, and the EU, for decades. For some unspecified reason, North Korea was not known to be an active participant. Majority of these states, possessed nuclear technology along with a stockpile of arms positioned to annihilate each other, restrained only by an awareness of MAD (mutually assured destruction), holding back by the merest thread (until only yesterday) the irreversible catastrophe of a totally devastated and uninhabitable planet.

I am Peter Glass, a Los Angeles businessman. My parents were émigrés from the Ukraine when the country became disorientated through Russian aggression. I took full advantage of the spate of Chinese acquisitions made in the USA over the past three decades to propel me out of poverty. As is well known, the Chinese independently developed space technology to such a level that they were able to compete, as equals, with the NASA space exploration program. There was then no other option than to cooperate in joint expeditions. My wife and I chose to fly into the International Space Station and learn about the scientific advances that space exploration offered. That was more than a holiday for us, it was our hobby. When she was alive, we used to make this trip every three years. Sadly, she died two years ago, and on this trip I acquiesced in her wish to have her ashes scattered across outer space.

I had been disillusioned with my earthly existence for quite some time. My wife died quite young, at the age of sixty-three, on 24th July 2044. This was death due to a genetic condition that sadly had we but been aware of in time, could well have avoided. Average life expectancy in most developed countries had risen to over 120 years in the last couple of decades.

Since all fossil fuel had been exhausted, we were fighting to preserve our dwindling share of water, wind, and the pathetically few reserves of cropland left. Several nuclear accidents had put a complete stop to the harnessing of nuclear power for everyday use. Most domesticated animals were being consumed to extinction. Wildlife could not avoid a similar fate. Terrorism resulting from various global antagonisms was rampant well before the nuclear apocalypse that human life was becoming rapidly unsustainable by the third decade of the twenty-first century.

Pollution and the resulting global warming created a plethora of hurricanes, floods, earthquakes and tsunamis over the last four decades, devastating many population centers and making millions homeless. Even wealthy nations were so overwhelmed that reparations were slow and ineffective. There was no international consensus on how to tackle the menacing problems of a runaway world.

Now, there is complete and utter silence from NASA and the other ground stations dotted around the world monitoring all the space stations and satellites in the sky. The two Chinese astronauts apprehended the situation as soon as they heard and sensed the earth's last dying tremors after several nuclear blasts formed mushroom clouds covering the entire visible surface of the earth. With wry smiles, they ceremoniously waved me goodbye, and took their last, unfettered space walk yesterday, minutes after the apocalypse.

I believe that the time has come for me to go the same way. I have nobody to wave goodbye to, so these notes must be considered my swansong. Perhaps the ISSIII module will be discovered by a future, more evolved species than us wretched and doomed *Homo sapiens.* If that happens, I may yet enter the hall of fame as one of the last space tourists from a once-flourishing planet, the third from the sun.

***

GOING HOME

The other day I called in at the local Police Station to report that my cat, Tabby, had been missing for over two days. I presumed it had been stolen. I left it until rather late in the day, indeed well past midnight, because I was celebrating a friend's birthday both at the local pub and at his home. Just before I was able to lodge my complaint, a policewoman escorting a strange looking elderly woman, sat her down in front of the enquiry desk. The woman looked so old that I was not surprised to see that she was prevailed upon to sit in a chair facing the duty Sergeant. Perhaps it was my semi-alert inebriation which helped to register what followed in such detail. A strange sequence of events, I am surprised that I could recall it later at all.

The old lady, (I almost referred to as the tramp), gave out an overpowering foul smell which emanated most likely from her ill-fitting, dirt encrusted clothes.

'You've been bought in for questioning. Found wandering the streets unable to explain your circumstances', the Sergeant intoned without even looking at her.

'What's your name?'

'Ford'

'Your first name?'

'Anglia'

The Sergeant eyed the woman for the first time and scowled.

'Look, don't play games with me. You'll spend the night in the slammer. Is that what you want?'

'I don't care where I spend the night'

'Are you homeless?'

'Not where I come from'

'Where's that?'

'Betelguese'

I was of course, eavesdropping. The woman was speaking English okay, but with a strange echo-like resonance. I vaguely remember having heard of such a place before, but couldn't be sure whether I had heard her right.

'Where the hell is that? Any papers ... Identification ...?'

'I don't carry anything. I don't have to. I just came for a quick visit'

'How long have you been here?'

'A couple of earth days, I reckon'

'What do you mean? Are you a refugee? Asylum seeker? Immigrant?

'Your policewoman called me a vagrant ... Call me what you like. It's all the same to me'

What is your date of birth?'

'No point. Not telling you. Won't make much sense even if I did'

'I warn you. You are making things difficult for yourself. Any relations ... family ... legal support, anyone we can contact?'

The woman took quite a bit of time to reply, but I gathered that she was trying to get across facts about her only brother being dead, and that he had lived here fifteen years before leaving in a hurry thinking that days on planet earth were numbered. She wanted to see for herself the terrain where her brother had spent his time on earth, although she was not one for nostalgia. She too was coming to the end of her natural life. She also said something about a trick played by mice with their own secret agenda, which while she was going on about it, made no sense to me.

'If the earth had perished, you wouldn't be sitting here now, would you?' she insisted.

A look of incredulity was creeping over the Sergeant's face.

'What was your brother's name?

'Ford. We are Fords, for formalities sake. He called himself Ford Prefect ... er ... not Prefect Ford.'

'Oh my God! You are talking of that researcher bloke in Hitchhiker's Gal ...aren't you? He was your brother?!!!'

'Exactly'

The Sergeant was now eyeing her with curiosity

'But wasn't that all fiction?'

The woman appeared rather disconcerted by the Sergeant's intent gaze.

'We don't use our senses like earthlings. See these eyes and ears, they are mere camouflage. I see and hear with my body. That's why I hate these bloody rags I had to pick up from a rubbish tip. I wear them only because if I didn't I may be stoned or apprehended and incarcerated without anything to cover myself. My nose is a complete fiction. The Betelguese olfactory sense is quite different.'

That explains it, I thought, because as I kept getting closer to the woman to hear her better, the evil smell continued to become more and more overpowering. Suddenly, I couldn't bear it any longer. Did it make me forget why I was there at the Police Station in the first place? I don't remember making a complaint about the loss of my precious pet.

As I turned away, did I hear the old woman scream that she was GOING HOME before darting out of the Police Station like a space shuttle launched from NASA? I sure did.

I rushed back home without any further thoughts about the fate of Anglia Ford or Ford Anglia, or whatever she called herself, I don't even remember going to bed before I woke up, late, fully dressed, with an almighty headache. Was I sloshed? ... that badly?

I drove straight down to my work place, although it was rather late in the day. Strangely enough nobody had noticed my absence. I decided not to speak to anyone about the previous night's experience, waiting to see, if and how the news media would report what appeared to me to be an 'out-of-this-world' event.

But then, most important, where the heck is my cat..... my poor cat?

***

HOW INCONVENIENT!

As a consequence of my losing balance and falling out of the bath while taking a shower, I caused the toilet bowl to be smashed into smithereens. As a result, for the last several months or so, plumbers and plumbing have been uppermost in my mind.

Even after two weeks off work on sick leave, my lower back around the waist still ached. The GP while signing the medical certificate was almost dismissive saying that I was lucky it was a mere muscular injury. I felt as if a giant had struck a blow across my waist from behind with an iron rod.

Painkillers didn't help that much. I didn't like taking them anyway. My wife, Sue, rubbed a supposedly soothing bottled balm, nightly over the first few days. It didn't stop her losing sleep due to my constant tossing and turning in bed. Finally, I settled for a hot water bottle. Not that it helped much either.

Luckily, we had an outdoor toilet on the ground floor facing the rear garden which catered adequately to our needs whilst awaiting replacement of the toilet in the main bathroom.

Although, when we first moved into this house, we had a specialist bathroom fitter to install the bathroom at enormous cost, we realised that nearing retirement age, we would not be able to secure a deal requiring regular monthly payments over several years into the future.

We therefore began scouring the local newspapers, Yellow Pages, and the Thompsons Directory, to locate bathroom fitters or suppliers. Our weekends were spent visiting local bathroom stores for replacement units.

Apart from the immediate and urgent necessity of replacing the completely demolished toilet bowl with another, we felt we needed to make a start by committing funds to buying at least one other item as an improvement to our old bathroom. The first item we thought of ordering was a vanity unit, with a wash basin and mirror. However, the unit came with an electric light as part of the package. For us, the central ceiling light had been quite adequate. We thought we would buy this unit and have it installed leaving out the non-essential mirror light.

We never imagined how difficult it was finding a plumber. Those who responded to our queries quoted exorbitant rates per hour, even though we were required to wait weeks before a plumber would deign to call and give us a firm quote and dates to undertake the work. We surmised that none of them was serious about taking on the job.

Three weeks after the vanity unit was delivered we thought we struck gold. A plumber would call Saturday morning between ten and twelve to look at the job, and if it was merely a case of just replacing an old unit with a new one, he would do it then and there. The rate was £60 per half-hour. Okay, not cheap, but we felt relieved. Saturday, we were expecting friends, a couple roughly our age, for dinner. But then, we could always take them out for a Chinese or Indian.

Saturday morning we were expectant – almost excited. Early morning I phoned the man we thought was the plumber to remind of his visit. He re-iterated that the appointment would be kept. Sharp at ten, when I telephoned again, the same voice answered.

'You are coming, aren't you?' I asked him bluntly.

'The plumber is on his way' the voice insisted. Obviously he was not the plumber. I had jumped to conclusions.

We waited until midday, but no plumber. At ten minutes past twelve, I dialled the phone number once again.

'The plumber hasn't come. You said between ten and twelve. It's gone twelve.'

'He's on his way. You got to wait.'

'For how long, though. He won't be able finish the job. We have people coming.'

'He'll be there.' He put the phone down.

My wife had overheard and was making faces indicating that she wasn't having any of it.

Half past one. Sue had rustled up a snack for lunch for the two of us. No plumber yet in sight.

What I had not foreseen was the difficulty, and in our case probably the near impossibility, of engaging a plumber to do what I thought was a simple, straightforward job. Lucrative long-term contracts were, I surmised, what they sought and thrived on. Unperturbed, perhaps even fatalistic, Sue began grilling a whole salmon for dinner. It was late afternoon. We were expecting our friends, the Kumars, for dinner.

At about half-past-four, the doorbell rang. We didn't expect the Kumars to come round that early. They were early diners, but even so, six-thirty was their usual dinnertime. As I opened the door, I glimpsed a man turning back towards a white van parked outside our home. It had a name followed by the words 'plumbing and heating' emblazoned across the side. A ruddy-cheeked man whipped round as the door opened.

'You have a job for me?'

'Ah, you are the plumber ...' Thought we agreed you'd come between ten and twelve.' I meant this as a mere conversation starter, not as a complaint.

'Do you want the job done or not?'

There was impatience or exasperation in his voice. With the door open he could see inside the house where the cardboard boxes containing the paraphernalia awaiting assembly in the bathroom lay scattered in the hallway.

'But ... but,' I could only stutter.

'Make up your mind. I've been working all day. No time to mess around.'

He was unnecessarily edgy, I thought. The next instant, he had turned his back on me and was inside the van.

'Let him go. We don't want **him.**' Sue was standing right behind me.

The van reversed with what I assumed was a snort and was gone in a flash.

Stupidly, I shouted after him. I have now forgotten what I uttered, but just as well, it is probably unrepeatable.

Our friends, when they arrived, had to negotiate their way around the boxes in the hallway. Not many minutes after dinner, saying their 'goodbyes' wriggling around the same boxes, the Kumars drowned my apologies crying in unison that the inconvenience was well worth it. The salmon and asparagus had been exquisite. Sue was pleased. Only I felt apologetic and somewhat crestfallen.

Sunday was the day I set apart for my weekly read of the Sunday Times while struggling, not always successfully, to complete the cryptic crossword. If I didn't finish it on Sunday, I could always come back to it during the week.

'Sue, take a look at this.'

Sue was slow to come to the lounge. Perhaps she thought I was going to pester her with an anagram I had trouble with. It was really a news item that attracted my attention.

'This guy has a first class honours degree and has ended up training as a plumber. He reckons he could make 75k a year in plumbing. Instead of wasting three years doing media studies Josh should have taken up plumbing.'

Josh was our 24 year old son. After getting his lower second-class degree from a post-polytechnic university, he was aimlessly adrift in the job market. While he flitted from job to job, he still remained anchored in his parental home. There was no likelihood of him taking up plumbing.

'Says here, Britain is short of 30,000 plumbers.'

'So, what chance do we have of getting our bathroom fixed?'

'Even less chance than winning the lottery.'

Well, that proved to be an exaggeration. Still, two months passed before we had someone recommend us a plumber. He agreed to fit all the units we had bought which were now cluttering the hallway. This man quoted around half the rate which others, perhaps not seriously interested in the job, had quoted. It was just within our budget, which had been revised upwards over the last couple of months.

Suddenly, my back started giving me trouble again, and I was allowed a few days off to get a second opinion. That was convenient. While my wife was away at work I would be at home while the plumbing began. Although the job was priced for four days, since he had brought another man with him, the plumber assured us that it would be completed in two days. How clever! It suited us fine. It was to be a cash-in-hand job and they wouldn't be bothered with clearing away the rubbish.

At Sue's suggestion I was assiduously to make tea three times a day to the exact requirements of the two plumbers. There was a Fortnum & Mason tin of biscuits that our dinner guests had brought with them. I believe that this perhaps was the first time ever that such a luxury item had found its way to our home. I felt that the plumbers deserved the treat at break time.

Since water was cut off from the mains, two bowls of water were kept in reserve. While the two men preferred tea, I made myself very strong coffee. It was better than taking painkillers. The two men went up and down the stairs bringing an arsenal of tools from their van. Sue had foreseen the likely mayhem and had laid down some old curtains as dust sheets on the stairs and landing.

Things went smoothly until the first tea break. That was when they hit a snag. The plug hole in the new bath was not in the same place as in the old bath and hence was not aligned with the waste pipe. They said they needed extra piping and I had to fork out more cash. Forty quid, they said. Before they left on the first day, they asked for more money to buy a sealant and other items not in my vocabulary or within my experience. They wanted to return a few coppers from their earlier purchase, but I waived this aside.

I felt lucky enough to have the job undertaken at last by two competent workmen. Before they started installing an item I heard them checking loudly with each other on what I took to be the appropriateness of their individual and joint actions. They also kept arguing about the effectiveness of each procedure, and at times perhaps made improvements at the second attempt. From my standpoint, such interpretations were necessary for me to reassure myself that all was well, that nothing was amiss.

I had forked out more than £60 on sundries over the agreed price before the job was finally completed. But, I was greatly relieved and more than happy that I joined them in their banter over the last occasion of our sitting down to tea and biscuits. Indeed, I felt so chuffed that I felt like laying it on a little.

'Plumbers are entitled to the best ... See, it's Fortnum & Mason.'

Silence. The boast couldn't have meant much to them.

'Call us, when you want the tiling done, mate.'

Cash paid, counted, and seen to be correct, we shake hands. The two men wave goodbye, and drive off in their van.

Time heals – so they say. Medication is not always benign. There are side-effects. However, I know there is no quick fix, but the pain has eased over time. My back needs time to heal by itself. Nature takes time to repair the old broken tissues and restore their function. At least, the weather is improving. I can expect to be my old self real soon. The enforced leisure break has done me good.

The old discarded bathroom suite, and debris of the smashed up fixtures and fittings lie strewn in our back garden in an untidy heap. I see the pile of junk crowned with the empty upturned Fortnum & Mason biscuit tin glistening merrily in the midday sun. Clearing up the mess would take time - a lot of my time – but this time, most assuredly, at my convenience.

***

PLANETARY EXTINCTION

The year is A.D. 2084, and we now live on a Unified Planet. Personally, this is my 100th year of existence, and at the most, I can expect to live another 25 years before my demise. That is the average life span at the end of the 21st century on earth.

In mid -21st century, when I was in my prime, the world was a very chaotic place. There was an information deluge with books, magazines, newspapers, discs, CDs, DVDs, MP3s, films and the Internet, pouring out an unregulated mass of mostly indigestible material in hundreds of languages. Today, it is different. Only the authorized, amongst which I am a recognized member, is allowed to propagate information sanctioned by the Elite. By A.D. 2075, at the beginning of our new world, once the Elite had taken total control, all unauthorized sources of information and entertainment were declared illegal, and ceased to exist almost overnight.

Now, the world languages are limited to four. Chinese, used by the largest proportion of the world's population, English, the next most widely used language, of which I am proficient, Spanish, another popular language, and to a lesser extent Arabic. Arabic is a minority language still used by those who originally opposed the complete abolition and annulment of world faiths, or religions, but managed to survive the nuclear disaster in the Middle East.

There was a growing consensus at the time within the United Nations, given the Human Rights ethos, that uncontrolled world pollution by lethal gas emissions, melting of the polar ice caps, population explosion, deforestation, species extinction, and the depletion of natural resources, was threatening the continued survival of the planet. Established religions with their fanatical adherents were also seen as obstacles to rational, science-based, human progress, and were outlawed.

The problem at the time was that with nearly 200 nation-states scattered across the globe, none was willing to take the lead in advancing drastic and conclusive measures to correct the global malaise. It was then, that the world's richest and most powerful trans-national, multi-national, conglomerates headed by enlightened men and women, concluded that there was no alternative but to take direct action. These rich, highly intelligent, and powerful individuals gathered in a colloquium, decided to override the interests of what were believed to be democratic, autonomous, industrialized nations, and take over the running of all planetary affairs. Among the powerful nation-states of the time were the People's Republic of China, the United States of America, and the Union of Europe, which after a rapid, violent upheaval in the mid-twenty-first century, came to include Eastern Europe and Russia.

Between A.D. 2070 and A.D.2075, while there was chaos in the Middle East, there were several, surreptitious, colloquia convened by around 250 of the richest, and most powerful multi-billionaires who controlled practically all of the earth's financial, manufacturing, and natural resources. All mineral, oil, gas, nuclear, wind, and solar energy were concentrated in the hands of these individuals, although nominally, some industrialized nation-states claimed partial ownership. They were also the beneficiaries of tax avoidance schemes which no state government could bring under control. All these powerful individuals were citizens of industrialized countries like the USA, Russia, China, Norway, Singapore and a few other nations with large reserves of capital and sovereign funds. Whatever their national and ethnic origins were, their desire for amelioration of the world's ills through world domination and unification, brought them together under one slogan a 'Unified Planet'.

These powerful individuals decided among themselves that nation-states had outlived their day and needed to be replaced by an enlightened cartel of those who controlled the world's resources. Multi-billionaires, all of them - some had already been named by scribes as 'philanthro-capitalists'.

In A.D. 2074 they finally went public. They had unanimously agreed that they, as a group, would take total political control of the world and turn it into a unified economy. None of them believed in the supernatural. They were opposed to all orthodox, established religious faiths. They held religions and tribal allegiances to be divisive and the cause of continuing armed conflict in the world. This powerful intelligentsia had by then sensed that the world's educated and influential individuals had developed a completely different belief system from the masses who were continuously being fed what their political masters thought were good for them. A powerful terrorist Islamic fundamentalist organization calling itself ISIL (Daesh), was totally wiped out through nuclear detonations even without recourse to Elite intervention.

The vast majority of the world's population was creatures under the surveillance of overt and covert Orwellian control systems adopted by the governing class. International espionage deploying the latest high-tech cyber communication tools was endemic. Although such terms were not used, it was evident that the masses were continuously being 'brainwashed" by the media with consumerism and popular culture used as the means of systematic indoctrination of individuals to conformity and submission in their daily lives.

The new intelligentsia now taking over the reins of world government saw a large proportion of the world's population as dispensable. Once the coup had been accomplished, and the political machinery of the world's powerful countries dismantled, it was easy for the Elite to put their policies into practice. They starved weak nations into complete submission and ensured the elimination of more than half the world's illiterate or semi-literate, indigent humans who were not conversant with Chinese, English, Spanish or Arabic. With such measures, they believed it possible to bring under control, and attenuate, fears of future conflicts, and total devastation of the earth.

The colloquium of the Elite, took steps to unify the whole of the English-speaking world, that is, North America, Canada, UK, Australia and New Zealand, as one political and economic system. Another group included Europe led by Russian oligarchs who took over the European Union, after its eventual collapse. Latin America along with the Iberian Peninsula was unified as Spanish speakers. The Orient, from India to Japan and China, but not including Australia and New Zealand was also brought under the hegemony of one political and economic system. The former Muslims, now debarred from practicing any form of that religion were eliminated, (if they hadn't been already) until only those who conformed to the new ethos were allowed to exist as one entity called Arabia. All affairs of state were conducted through a system of voluntary committees and sub-committees of the Elite in each of the four regions. The Elite had no difficulty in equitably allocating and distributing financial and other resources among and between themselves through mutual agreement.

Those among the Elite who believe that they have reached retirement age are able to migrate to space colonies dotted around the earth's stratosphere. Mars and Venus have already been colonized and open to settlement by earthlings. Regular interplanetary travel has become a matter of routine. Members of the Elite, who retire, nominate their successors from among the up-and-coming entrepreneurs in their respective fields. There are large seagoing vessels or ocean liners that perform the function of luxury hotels which accommodate the Elite and their retinue of followers and staff.

As noted above, there are only four languages designated as official languages which are: Chinese, English, Spanish and Arabic. The Elite developed the facility for instant translation from one language to another. Hence communication between and among those belonging to the intelligentsia from diverse ethnic and linguistic backgrounds has never been a problem.

Although libraries exist, there are no new publications, unless sanctioned by the Elite. Instant information dissemination via satellite and large television screens installed in every household has become the standard means of keeping the populace up-to-date on events of importance. There is no longer any wasteful currency speculation as the Elite adopted a single planetary currency, the Wuro. Almost all payments are made using an app on mobile phones, with coins, centimes or Wuro notes of any denomination soon becoming obsolete. Debt of any kind, corporate or individual, is no longer deemed necessary in any type of financial transaction. All transactions are up front and involve cash or capital transfers through the one and only World Bank with branches all over the world.

All forms of violence hitherto depicted as entertainment in the cinema was abolished and the film industry as we knew it in the past, has ceased to exist. Smoking was banned, the tobacco companies taken over, and their assets stripped to be put to alternative use. The use of alcohol is permitted but rationed and restricted. Large sums of money spent on scientific research on possible cures for long-standing incurable diseases were curtailed, and sufferers of such diseases allowed the practice of euthanasia, which is now entirely within the law. It was no easy matter to dismantle the massive drug manufacturing industry of the past. Natural remedies are the new norm.

The motor vehicle industry too had been getting out of hand since the mid-21st century, and the Elite imposed quotas on the world's vehicle manufacturers. Since some of the original vehicle manufacturers were members of the Elite, the quotas were mutually agreed and rigorously imposed. All vehicles are now powered by electricity or hydrogen, fully automatic, and driverless. The proliferation of flying cars has eased traffic congestion in almost all big cities.

Since there is no longer any need for general elections, and subsequently a need to keep the masses happy and ignorant with fake news, the necessity for idolized celebrities either from the sports field or the entertainment industry has faded. Pop music and drug use are considered unnecessary and counter-productive that these are banned and, it is envisaged, will disappear totally. There are ample, well-attended sporting events and musical concerts without the hysteria associated with such events in the past.

People take many more holidays than in the past, often travelling to distant places for their vacations. There is constant travelling around from one part of the globe to another, by air, sea and land. Travelers are suitably entertained. Regular space travel is also encouraged.

There is no permanent institution of marriage. People are free to form liaisons at will, the only restriction being that children from all such liaisons should not exceed two in number. LBGT is tolerated although not actively encouraged. Pedophilia and pornography are ruthlessly suppressed through imposing severe penalties including the death sentence. Children are brought up and educated by a designated state apparatus. The Elite has provided for the nurture and education of all children through centralized nurseries, schools and academies. University education is provided free for the brightest five percent of the population and the others are directed early towards training and apprenticeships in careers most suited to their individual talents. There is no unemployment, in that those deemed unemployable for whatever reason, are humanely eliminated. The Elite ensures that population growth is kept well under control. The working week has been set at four days and the hours worked agreed individually with each employee as standard practice.

Initially, the greatest threat to the unity of the cartel came from arms manufacturers. Although wars had been made unnecessary and irrelevant, it was extremely difficult to decommission the arsenal of deadly weapons including nuclear warheads that the world's military had accumulated. The consensus was strong that they should diversify. Gradually, the arms manufacturers were won over and have since been putting their skills to peaceful use including space exploration. Indeed, this is proving a wise move as regular trips are undertaken to Mars and Venus with large, viable, human settlements forming on these planets. These ventures have helped to more than recoup the initial losses suffered due to the absence of arms sales.

Once the world's nuclear arsenal was decommissioned, nuclear fission is being harnessed for peaceful purposes with adequate provision for waste disposal. Although the four major regions of the world, the English-speakers, the Orient, Spanish speakers, and the much smaller Arabia retain independent police forces, there are no longer any standing armies, navies, or air forces since there is no cause for conflict following the unification of the world, politically and economically.

Business corporations or conglomerates do not strive for bottom line profits. Increasingly the monetary value of goods and services has become meaningless in a unified world economy. There is enough to go round, and no dearth of essential commodities. Delivery systems are automated and extremely efficient. Excellence, achievement, and innovation, in any field of human endeavor are rewarded by public recognition accorded to the individual or team. Almost all industrial and menial tasks are performed by robots. Artificial Intelligence ranks high on the educational ladder with a wide-ranging and rapidly evolving syllabus.

Over the last few years there has been a spectacular reduction in crime. Prisons are beginning to become redundant and most are being converted into hospices and schools. The residue of those engaging in criminal activity is seen as mentally and emotionally disturbed, and are isolated, but cared for. There is though, provision for the total, humane elimination of those in psychiatric care, if the prognosis continues to be negative. These measures are designed to ensure the healthy genetic endowment of future generations.

These notes are to be archived so that future historians will be enabled to get a true picture of the momentous changes that occurred towards the end of the 21st century, giving birth to the new era of the Unified Planet.

(Sgd. Illegible)

Corrigendum

The date is 21st December 2104. I am not the writer of the exaggeratedly glowing account of the state of affairs in the world as described above. His name and rank are omitted from this report. I am most likely the only surviving member of the human race living close to earth today. Almost all fit and healthy surviving earthlings have moved to, and are now occupying Mars and Venus. As the Supreme Space Scientist, I have been based at the Omega Space Station in orbit for the last five decades. More recently I have worked alone here with no assistants. However, before I depart from the orbit of this planet forever, and retire to my pad in Venus, I feel the need to put things straight on record.

Almost immediately, before the Elite took over the reins of world government, a series of earth shattering events took place in the Middle East. Indeed, it was these events that precipitated the take-over bid by the colloquium of capitalists in whose hands were concentrated the greatest proportion of the world's wealth and resources.

The endemic Shia-Sunni conflict spread among all Muslim countries in the Middle East resulting in an all-out nuclear war. It extended from Pakistan, and the Muslim states of the former Soviet Union in the north-east, to the Emirates and Yemen in the south and Turkey to the west. Afghanistan, Iraq, Iran, Syria, Egypt, Jordan, Lebanon, Palestine, Saudi Arabia, Libya, Tunisia, Algeria, Morocco, Kenya, Nigeria, Ethiopia, Eritrea, Mali, and other African countries with a substantial Muslim population, were unable to stand aside from the conflict. Israel too could not escape the conflagration. Of the bordering European countries, Greece and most of the islands of the Mediterranean, had the misfortune of being situated in the midst of the war zone and was wiped out.

Nobody was able to produce a verifiable account of what exactly happened and how and when it all started. What is known is that towards the end of 2070 the region experienced nuclear detonations which resulted in several Chernobyls and Fukushimas leaving the whole of the Middle East and the adjoining Western states in total meltdown. No one from outside the devastated areas of the earth was able to track and assess the extent of the catastrophe. A few drones sent by the former USA attempted to map the area, but the multiple mushroom clouds prevented any real intervention.

The Elite imposed a ban on all attempts to explore the region. By confining and cordoning off the nuclear devastated region of the earth, the Elite believed that it remain an object lesson to the planet's survivors. However, it was an illusion to believe that the rest of the earth's surface including the oceans would not, in the end, be affected by radioactive contamination.

As a mouthpiece for the Elite, the writer of the piece above clearly intended the populace to remain ignorant of these true but unsavory facts.

Although it took more than three decades, it has finally happened. The planet earth gradually became totally uninhabitable, and the prognosis is that it would remain so for an incalculable period of time into the future. Thankfully, from the depleted earth's population, all those who could manage it, have already departed to the welcoming colonies of Mars and Venus. At the sad and final end to their world, do the surviving *homo sapiens* keep asking themselves; 'Is there still no place like home?

Signed: Supreme Space Scientist of the former planet Earth.

***

THE TOUR GUIDE

Before the economic crisis of 2008, you wouldn't have failed to come across organized day tours in this part of Spain, known as 'blanket trips' offered entirely free of charge. You could sign up for a blanket trip at any one of the street markets local to you. These trips were promotions for 'merino' lamb wool products, mostly mattresses, pillows and blankets. No one was compelled to buy any items, but it was imperative that everyone attend the presentation extolling the virtues of merino wool bedding. Invariably one or two people would be tempted to buy some of these products, and even with only a couple of buyers the organizers would have been able to realize a fair return for their efforts.

There were also (and still are) a couple of private coach firms advertising day trips at reasonable prices, some of them including lunch. There are a number of interesting coastal and inland towns and villages accessible on such day trips. All the coaches, as of necessity, have a driver and a tour guide.

It is the role of the tour guide which interests me. She is, invariably a middle-aged English-speaking lady, who tries to keep you entertained while on the coach. She is a mine of information, and can churn out an interesting spiel spiced with risqué jokes. My wife and I have done quite a few trips, but the trips to Guadalest were the most memorable, both as free 'blanket trips' and paid coach trips.

There are various pick-up points for passengers on the way to these locations. When all the passengers are comfortably seated, the guide is ready to welcome and address the passengers. She introduces the driver and gives her own name. By this time we could be passing Santa Pola, on route N332. She describes the origin of the salt marshes, and relates what you can expect to see at the salt museum. She points to the possibility of us seeing flamingos, and we could be straining our necks to glimpse a couple far away in the distance. The watchtower that finally succeeded in keeping the Berber pirates from attacking the village is pointed out. It has been renovated from the outside recently, she explains. The guide then describes Guadalest as the second most visited tourist attraction in Spain, second only to the Royal Palace in Madrid.

As the next item of interest she points to the large outline of a black bull on a bill-board some distance away from the road. I was intrigued to learn that it had originally been an advertisement for a local brand of brandy. At the time, it happened to be a colorful roadside bill-board, which, they say, distracted motorists, occasioning many accidents. The government banned it, but popular sentiment ensured its retention in the present blacked out form, no longer advertising anything other than that it is a Spanish icon. Taurus is an impressive symbol of Spain, the home of bull-fighting.

On the way to Guadalest, now on AP 7 (motorway), we pass the famous James Bond actor Roger Moore's former holiday home painted an eye-catching blue. There is also the range of mountains referred to as the 'Sleeping Indian'. You have to stretch your imagination to see the outline of a supine Red Indian wearing the traditional headdress in the outline of the mountain range. Another story our guide tells us is that of the legend of a giant rebuffed by an Arabian princess. In his pique, he broke off a bit of the mountain and threw it in the sea, which formed the island, Isla de Tabarca. 'If you believe that, you'll believe anything' she adds. She also has a story about the differently coloured houses in the coastal town of Villajoyosa. When the fishermen come ashore with their catch, they are in a hurry to get drunk at any one of the nearby inns. Their wives dress them in shirts matching the colour of their houses, and even if they are quite 'non compos mentis' with gallons of alcohol inside them, it is said that they can all be directed towards the right house and into the arms of the right spouse, thanks to the colour-coding of the houses.

On the 'blanket trips' there are sometimes items for sale inside the coach, and on the return trip, a lottery draw for some item that nobody probably ever thinks of buying. Inevitably, it is in aid of some charity or other. On paid coach trips, there is always the need to sell the idea of another, different trip next time. Often, on the return journey, most passengers are comatose with too much food and drink inside them, and are allowed to snooze without much chatter from the guide. At this point she might remind us that the Spanish drivers are paid so little that a small, or even a generous tip, would be most welcome.

As a parting gesture the tour guide recounts a risqué joke (about three nuns and St Peter) that wakes everyone out of their slumber guffawing. A slightly more repeatable joke is about a new customer at a restaurant, intrigued by what people at the next table were eating, asking to be served the same dish. The waiter apologizes and says that there is only a limited supply from the bull ring, and asks the customer to book a table for another day. When he returns, he is served a small-scale version of the dish he had seen before. He is somewhat put off, and asks why there's this difference. The waiter responds by asking the customer; 'you wouldn't expect the matador to win every time, would you?' Sadly, 'blanket trips' have now disappeared from the scene.

This is the sort of life retired expatriates like us who live in Spain enjoy. They know that they do not have many more years ahead of them, and want to have innocent fun, while living here in the Costas.

***

WHO IS SHE?

Oh! Hello. Did you say something about a name plate? The editor of the 'Daily Bleeper' doesn't believe in name plates or identity tags. Okay. Let me introduce myself. I am Naomi Bassey... No, no! No relation at all. Wish I had made all that money without having to risk life and limb. Or, be her daughter, and have some of the lolly left to me.

No, my parents were said to have come from Somalia, or perhaps even Sierra Leone. Not sure. I suppose they were refugees, or even illegal immigrants. Who knows? Didn't get to know anything about them before they disappeared from my life altogether. I doubt if Bassey was their real name either. Yes. I was adopted as a baby. My adoptive parents were – wait for it - Smiths. Pity. I no longer have any contact with them either. I must admit there was a time when I desperately wanted to know who I was.

Hey!!! Don't feel sorry for me. I am not complaining. The Smiths provided me with a good home. I was one of the first to go to university from our Comprehensive. I made good friends at Uni. I met my boyfriend Jamal there. We only got back just over a year ago after a post-university gap year jaunt around the world. Fabulous, I tell you. Yes, Jamal is my fiancé now. Look at this gorgeous ring he gave me just last week.

Why am I sitting here? Editor's decision. She always comes up with these wacky promotional schemes. Making a statement for equal opportunities? How corny is that? I am female; I am black, if anybody cares to notice. I don't want to be anybody's 'token'. I got this job squarely on merit. Eighteen months now. Ask my colleagues. Well, of course, one or two might be a wee bit jealous. That's office life for you. No, this is not my normal work station. I often work from home, on my laptop, bringing my work in a memory stick to the office once a week, and downloading it all into the office computer. I share a hot desk with two others.

My normal work tools are not paper and pen, or pencil. I can hardly read my own handwriting. I prefer to get my thoughts down straight on to the laptop via the keyboard. I use a lead pencil only when I do crosswords. I can't resist cryptic crosswords.

Although you may think I am idling on company time, Rebecca doesn't think so. For her, this is great PR work. I hope you don't mind my saying that there are quite a few of you who make their way straight to the wine and canapes, and really don't care a damn about much else that is going on here. Our editor, Rebecca, still thinks it worthwhile to show the 'human face' of what today's paparazzi are about. I suppose that's why she puts on this kind of road show at the 'Daily Bleeper' once in a while.

I am here from eight in the morning until one in the afternoon. One of my colleagues Sheila will cover the one-to-five shift. No, no, this is not all I do for the newspaper. Surely, you must have read my weekly column. Oh, I forgot, I sign my column Vassie de Silva, my nom-de-plume, not as plain old Naomi Bassey. So, now you know.

Hold it! Hold it! There's a 'Suggestion Box' downstairs, on your way out. You can make your views known to all and sundry. Or, you can write to the editor, as usual. I guess you are all regular readers of 'The Daily Bleeper' and 'The Sunday Bleeper' or else you wouldn't bother to be here, would you? Well, that's a big assumption, isn't it? Oh alright!. You are the very well-informed general public who are also our supporters and advertisers. So, here we are, showing you our human side. Authenticity is a b-e-e-g buzz word around here. But, as you may well be aware, we journalists are forced to hide behind masks some of the time.

We do a lot of community support work. We invite school-kids to come over on special days and shadow our sub-editors, reporters, illustrators, photographers – the whole darn lot. Wish I had that in my time. I was thrown in at the deep end. Sink or swim. Good thing that I was born with that tribal .stubbornness, foolhardiness, whatever you may care to call it. I like to think that my ancestors killed lions with their spears for sport, or at their initiation ceremonies. Yes, one day I might do just that. No, not kill lions. I mean … go in search of my origins, roots, like .,. Who was it? Kunta Kinte did? If I remember right, it was all a load of baloney, wasn't it? Do we ever really know who we are?

Thank you. You like my dress. Which girl doesn't love designer outfits? I shop at Miramar as often as I can. How long will I be able to keep doing that, I don't know. Oh, .no!

I am not expecting to be made redundant, or given the sack. I am more worried about being posted abroad. One of these days, I might end up in Syria or some other hotspot as special correspondent. You could bet on that. Did you know that at least one hundred journalists lost their lives in the first six months of war in Iraq and Afghanistan? Abduction could be a fate worse than death. So they say, but preferable, I say, if you are lucky enough to survive, you have a good story to tell, and the chance of becoming a celebrity.

No, seriously, people don't seem to understand or appreciate the price we pay for our freedom. I am sure you have heard of Anna Politkovskaya, the Russian journalist who ultimately paid with her life for telling the truth. Fortunately, we can still consider ourselves safe in this part of the world, but for how long? I wonder? A bullet with your name on it could be just around the corner.

Sh! But I do have a Plan B. The idea came to Jamal and me at the same time while we were spending a few days of our holiday on a Thai island. No, Phuket is not the only island in Thailand! This is a very obscure little place. I won't even care to name it, if you see what I mean. This is a place where those of us tired of the rat race go and downsize, or downshift, whatever. So, less people know about it the better.

You ask me: What are you tired of? You've only just started'. I must admit that you have a point. My answer is that my generation is far more worldly-wise than was yours. In the 21st century our world has shrunk. In the past people believed in something greater than themselves. Now all that is left is dog-eat-dog, grabbing more and more at someone else's expense.

We talk of nations, communities, people, but all we have left are coalitions of power. Less than one percent of the population are amassing riches driven by nothing more than greed and avarice. The rich get richer by being tax-dodgers. No one cares. All they seek to do is muzzle the press. We pay lip-service to high ideals, democracy, equality, liberal values, but even our high profile charities are nothing but a cover for naked self-interest.

Meanwhile, I write my weekly column on the antics of fashionable youth in this maelstrom.

Oh my god! Are they all of a sudden leaving? Was I boring you? No matter. I wasn't joking when I spoke about a Plan B.I think Jamal and I have enough between us to get to that island. That's far better than being martyred in Syria or Myanmar. But, come to think of it, I'll miss the occasional shopping at Miramar, dining at the Blitz, not to mention dancing at the Funky Buddha.

'POLICE! Don't move!

"Naomi Bassey, alias Vassie de Silva, I am arresting you on a charge of aiding and abetting terrorists under the Prevention of Terrorism Act 2003, by engaging in a coded dialogue with Daesh operatives in Manchester using your column 'Wry Comments' in 'The Daily Bleeper'. You have the right to remain silent, but anything you say will be taken down and used in evidence in a court of law."

Is this some kind of joke? Terrorists!!!

I thought I was exploring the depths of a hidden facet of my inner self by goofing around with a gang of pretentious pranksters. Now, it's come to this. How awful!!!

***

THE YOUNG MAN WITH TWITCHING EYES

A nerve-racking depression produced by a succession of indeterminate illnesses had gripped me in a deathly torpor. Yet, to almost everybody in my village, I was the lad enjoying an enviable and unjustified leisure. The villagers dug for gems in pits filled with muddy water, tapped rubber trees for latex in the drizzly mornings, clung on to rolling bullock carts down steep inclines, and spent a day at the hospital with their sick offspring. Their women lined the co-operative store for the weekly rations. Evening saw them bound for home with many a load on their heads and limbs.

I was reasonably well for a day or two between two bouts of illness. I would then transfer all my strength to my feet and trudge a four mile distance to town. A few villagers broke the 'thud', 'thud' rhythm of my well shod feet to throw a word or two at me beneath their familiar smiles. To them, I had cultivated the habit of answering affably and courteously.

Wiry young peasants waiting for hours for the one overcrowded bus to take them to town expressed loud disgust at it and began walking in my wake.

'My God! I can never stand suffocation inside that little bus, that's why I prefer walking' I would remark on these occasions swinging myself up to an authoritative height. The short, wiry peasants were often impressed and asked me whether I worked at the post office. 'Oh no, unless I passed all my examinations I wouldn't consider myself for any job', I told them. 'In fact I was awaiting the results of an examination that very week'. I reflected on how in the bus I had to crane my neck above the suffocating and sweat-reeking mass pressed like hens in a closed pen.

The road clambered past up the neat rubber estates out into the open valley of paddy fields. A russet uniformity framed by green *Wetakeya* leaves across the road announced that harvest time was drawing near. Rain had done a good deal of harm to the crops. Exactly how I did not know. The farmers could not enlighten me. In the distance, a harvest-gathering could be seen. But the chanting voices were uniformly old and feeble. I imagined sadly what a grand ritual this ought to have been with the joyous mixing of fresh and young voices with the old and feeble. That was an indispensable characteristic of a harvest.

'In Kandy paddy transplanting is a regular feature; the plant grows very tall there and you ought to see the number of people gathered at a harvest', I told the farmers. Nobody would care to trouble themselves about transplanting when it was not worth the expense they told me. I felt guilty about bringing up the subject. Then I thought of myself as a child in a remote village near Kandy. I had a place there. I wasn't a foreign presence, not an object of irritation, like the inevitable thorn. I was seven or eight then and I remember myself inside a *Kamatha* in the fields of a friendly and benevolent neighbour. I ran and danced with the smell of paddy and the voices of other children intoxicating my brain. I helped them thresh paddy far into the moon-lit night. I circled the *Kamatha* behind the knowing bulls with stick in hand over the gathered paddy, though the beasts did their job with the least bidding and without undue excitement. A little straw-thatched hut on one side of the *Kamatha* was a pavilion for our neighbour's children. With the roughness of the new straw, they had enough use of both hands to scratch themselves. Nevertheless, harvesting was a celebration, a ceremony. It was all such a dull affair now. How many were the wretches now debarred from this age-old ritual of rejuvenation, energy and life. I bowed my head while the sun bothered me in a merciless heat-ecstasy.

My friend, the young man with twitching eyes, lived a few yards away from the centre of the town. Though I call him a young man he was well past his thirties and was far from being the steady old bachelor. He was trying to establish himself as a teacher of English for the village lads. He wanted me to teach them arithmetic. My acquaintance with math, I told him, wasn't an entirely happy one. I had not worked at a sum for three years since I sat for my last examination with arithmetic as a subject. However, I agreed to teach arithmetic and gave three lessons in which I was compelled to work a large number of sums which by some miracle all came right. But, struggling with convoluted examples in arithmetic did not make me very comfortable. I decided to give it up.

'You know my mother does not like you very much. She doesn't want me coming here.'

'Hm! I have felt that she definitely hates me. What's the reason, I wonder?' the young man started twitching his eyes.

'She says you are poor and unsuccessful!'

'Poor! What does she know about me? Does she know that …..'

'She says you have failed examinations; that you are a total failure'.

'Be careful, she is possessive and jealous. Some trouble with her emotional adjustment. Your father cannot play the role she expects from him. She has turned on you'.

'I think I understand. But what can I do. I feel myself totally abandoned'.

'There you go. Pull yourself together man. Don't let others live your life for you. You know you have your intellect to your credit. Just look at the photograph of this minister in today's newspaper. I used to know him from the time we were at college. He is as mediocre as a miracle nowadays. What do you think he will do in this Commission? He will refer to some Buddhist scriptures to find out what aspect of life can best be exploited to create a public outcry….'

'I am sort of scared you know. I feel crushed by everybody. I feel suffocated like being in an overcrowded bus. And now I cannot even believe your words. I think all this time I had been pepped up for no reason. This is an age of standardization. Is there any reason why one shouldn't stick to the efficient standard product when a luxury article would mean more expense in repair and maintenance?'

'Don't worry; we can device the spare parts and it will be a joy for the engineers to do a spot of original work with your luxury article.

And …don't you put any faith in anything outside you? Society loves its failures.'

My friend was now twitching all over. He had been walking up and down the room. Occasionally he looked up as if he was in a sublime mood. Yet he had that nervous symptom of a regular twitch in his eyes and pouting of his mouth that did not go well with his deportment.

I remarked how well he had looked in the white suit and dark blue tie at some public function we both attended. He had not noticed me there. I did not feel that he was posing or trying to impress. 'I was a damn good cadet in my school days' he told me.

'I'll make a cup of tea for you', he said and screwed up his eyes at the kerosene stove in a corner of the room. It gave out a vermilion flame which he adjusted to Prussian blue. He took out the kettle and poured some hot water into a jug with some tea leaves in it.

On his table the alarm clock showed that it was nearly twelve o' clock. I told my friend that it was time for me to leave. He wanted me to stay for lunch. I refused. He then asked me to come on Saturday to have lunch with him. I agreed.

'My new assistant-cum-secretary will also be here. You know, we must ensure that she doesn't flirt too much. That's why I want you too to be there' and he twitched his eyes in an unintended mocking grimace.

'I am glad that you've taken to her'. I said as I placed on the table the cup of tea I had been sipping.

I came back Saturday. I was shown to my friend's elderly mother who had come to stay with her son. She was in bed, evidently an invalid. The girl, the secretary, looked gloomy and was seriously bent over her work.

'Why, has she flirted again' I asked my bachelor friend.

'Yes, by Oedipus and God, she has', he exclaimed and started twitching his eyes.

***

LONDON LIFE

It is windy and raining hard. Two men rush inside the café for 'fair trade' coffee.

'I still don't know your name?'

'Call me Archie … ! Don't know why … people laugh when I say my full ... my ... real name'.

'Well, what **is** your name? You know I won't laugh at **you**'.

Oh, ... It's Archimedes'.

'I see ...good – famous name. I didn't laugh, did I?'

'You... nice man. Not like others.'

'Okay Archie – you said you didn't like talking much about the past. Like … what happened back home. Is that still the case? Are you still reluctant to talk about what happened?'

'What's the point man, all bad … terrible … not like here … cops, prison, torture. Want to forget. Only good thing was football. Just a few good years… Hopeless… Can't play no more'.

'Why can't you play football now?'

'No way ... my leg bad ... still hurts ...'.

'Oh .. I see... I'm sorry... You settling okay ... otherwise?'

'Settling? … no proper job yet'.

'Remind me, what have you been doing recently?'

'Not much … two hours week visit mentally ill guy. Go shopping with him. Earn few bob ... as volunteer.'

The two men keep chatting. A getting to know chat with Archie replying to questions put by his counsellor, Mike.

It is still raining outside.

'Another coffee?

'I get it … okay?

Archie shuffles across to the counter; raises two fingers. 'Two more coffee .. please … Ow much?'

'You can have refills free'.

'Yeah? Cool! You hear that Mike? It's FREE!'

Archie gets back to his seat. The waiter follows him and pours more coffee into the two mugs. Mike only wants his mug half filled. He drops a lump of sugar in the mug and stirs.

It is now less of a downpour and more of a drizzle outside, but the wind has not abated. Litter lifts and shuffles in unruly clumps across a winding street in East London.

'Archie, you speak good English.'

'Thank you Mike, you very kind. What I picked up as refugee in this country.'

'Hm! So … what do you do with this guy you see? Two hours a week you say? Talk much?'

'Not for long time. Suddenly, he start … then, chat …chat …. Most times we go to post office, cash his Giro … then shop at Tesco. Walk back. Two hours gone. I go home to my digs'.

'Ah! Now I remember, Vanessa, your Centre Director, … she told me you ought to have helped Raman decorate his flat.'

'Yea, paper wall, carpet floor, she say. She gives half, but Raman must put half – that's the deal.'

'So, what happened?

Nothing. Raman lazy. He don't want nothing. He like zombie.'

'Why do you think he's like that?'

'Injections every month. He tell them reduce. They say he need more. Nobody listens to him!'

'Well I'd have thought that the shrinks know best. What can you do? They say Raman is schizophrenic, whatever that is. He must take his medicine'.

'Drugged to eyeballs!'. Archie slaps his forehead with both hands.

'Has he got friends, relations?

'In India … maybe. But parents dead. They brought him over when 12 year old, he tell me. You know Mike, I never met anyone from other side of the world, until I met Raman … in London!'

'In this country he is lucky. He gets welfare benefits as a permanently ill, disabled man.'

'Don't know about that ... not much of a life, has he? He say he liked very much working – minicabbing. He say he definitely not mad... no way!'

'Okay. ...minicab driver, was that what he did before he became ill?

'Oh yea, about ten year before, he tell me he bought brand new car, cash, because he sold shop in Midlands and come to London. Share of family shop – something like that'.

'Did he really? Who would have guessed?

'They burned it. New car. On the estate here. His woman, English? Irish? whatever. Sleeping with other men. Set them up to it. Insurance don't pay. No way he can earn money.

'He had a wife?

'No marry. Living both together. One son, he say. Don't see over ten years. Don't care.'

'Well, he had good reason to go mad'.

'Mad ..., angry, but no crazy. That's what he say. He never crazy.'

'He went to Jobcentre ask benefit. He pay no tax. So, no dole, they say. No money. Nobody care. So, he go mad – angry - at Jobcentre'.

'Did he?

'Just shouting loud he say, but no violence, he swear.'

'What happened?

'They call police. He keep on shouting. Say to police, you can't arrest me. What charge?

'Then…?

'Cops drag him away to police station. He ask where you taking me? They say, You'll see. They tell him we can make you 'psycho'. He, six-footer. Punjabi – big Indian. Police take him to hospital.

By the way, his ancestor in British Army, won Victoria Cross medal – I see picture in his flat.'

'They sat on him – five coppers. Doc give injection. He knocked out. Then, everyday injection – injection. In hospital bed for one year. Hostel after that, two year more, now at last he got council one-bed flat. Alone, he has no one. He given up.'

'Oh well, at least he's now got the state hand-out he asked for in the first place, hasn't he? Even more lolly now, I suppose. And, don't forget - for the rest of his life.'

Yeah? You can do that here?

'But this is no good, Archie. You ought to get a proper job!' Mike looks hard at Archie, as if appraising him. 'I'll help you with your CV.'

The two men both drain their coffee mugs at the same time.

The rain has stopped completely. Archie and his counsellor leave the café, still talking. The detritus in the London streets around them keep piling up.

THE REUNION

I ran into Colvin, I think – probably after more than thirty years. He was the only Carribean guy I could think of as a friend in those uprooted, nomadic days of our youth that in our different ways, were given to self-conscious, rebellious, anti-establishment posturing. Even so, comparing notes later, I was surprised to learn that he was my junior by almost a decade. I must have been exceptionally retarded and slow to grow up – if, I ever did grow up. There he was crossing over to the park bench where I had been sitting and ruminating for the better part of an hour.

After the Beatles, Mohamed Ali, Castro and Che Guevara, I remember only vaguely someone called Cohn Bendit, holding any fascination for us in the Sixties.

Among the female sex, I remember Twiggy, Joan Baez, Mary Quant and Germaine Greer as making an impact in their separate ways. Looking back, only the most politicised among us would have been actively concerned with 'apartheid' or, at that time its shadowy victim Nelson Mandela. Although much in the news, Martin Luther King Jr inspired very few among us blacks or browns in Britain. Che Guevara, unfortunately was appropriated early enough as a trademark icon of youth culture by the media. As far as I can remember Colvin was the most 'with it' lad among a lot of us nonentities who may have bothered to express concern over Mandela's fate, or Malcolm X being debarred from entering Britain.

I couldn't believe my eyes. Although greying, Colvin appeared to have a full head of hair with an untypically bourgeois countenance Was that a briefcase he was carrying? Even though he seemed to be in a hurry, he stopped dead in his tracks as soon as he saw me. I had never seen him in a full suit before. I stood staring at him unsure whether this was indeed Colvin.

'What you doing, man? You live around here?'

None of the warmth of recognition, or fellow feeling one expects from an old friend.

'At the moment – yes. No fixed abode and not much to do, but the Freedom Pass is a help.'

Seeing him still looking vague and distant, I added by way of explanation: 'not much has happened since those Chalk Farm days - surviving. And you?'

This was not the Colvin I knew. He sounded impatient and abrupt. 'Come to Lonchester chapel, Sunday. I'll give you the low-down then. Er... no need to dress up. Come as you are.'

His speech was markedly different. There was more than a hint of formality, I thought. He had rapidly glanced over my grimy sweatshirt, frayed corduroys and the muddy pair of trainers. I had to hang on to them as long as possible, before I felt able to afford another visit to the launderette.

'Colvin, you, a churchgoer?' Goodness! You've come a long way since your solidarity speeches addressing the ducks in Regent's Park!'

'Come to church Sunday before ten. Must hurry - meeting.'

My surprise was such that I could not formulate quickly enough what to say in reply – and, he was gone. While I was never more than on the fringes of whatever was going on in those days, Colvin was a firebrand Marxist who preached that religion was the equivalent of a trendy marijuana joint, if not exactly the 'opium of the people.'

That Sunday in early spring, with the sun promising to break through, I made my way to the Lonchster chapel for want of better things to do. I felt that, had Colvin been still the friend I thought he was, he would have invited me to his home or pad. That was the way we did things in those days. Your digs were as good as mine when we needed a place to park ourselves.

Still, some lingering affection overrode my sensitivity to what I thought was his rudeness.

The church hall next to the chapel was full of clusters of chattering men and women of varied age, size, and ethnicity. The familiar smell of detergent in the air suggested clinical cleanliness.

I soon learnt that Colvin was married with three kids. Doing okay, all in, or just out of university. Colvin was involved in some sort of import-export business. Wife had a steady job in the Civil Service, and I suspected that she was the financial mainstay of the family. I realised that a visit to his home without prior notice would prove tricky. In any case, Colvin was now a pillar of the community. And I – I was still an old bachelor, never having made anything of myself. Mind you, Colvin wasn't boasting, or anything like that. Even from my point of view, he had merely got round to doing the things that most people feel that they are here in this world to do, and was very obviously proud of what he had achieved. How many of us can remain lifelong revolutionaries and make a career of it? Even Cohn Bendit was said to have sold out and joined the bourgeoisie.

Solitary musings have always been a feature of my life. Now they were taking the following form. 'Look at the old Soviet Union, Red China, and even Cuba. Who would now believe that the Third World War was imminent over Cuba?'

WW3 would have been the end of the planet as we know it. Good God! That certainly would have been the END. Not a single soul left to commemorate the end of a full planetary apocalypse! I had never been a 'revolutionary'. Just a has-been of nothing – really

Over the years most of our 'fellow travellers' succumbed to illnesses, mental and physical. Largely undiagnosed and untreated, they had simply ceased to exist on earth. As for me, I was quite hale and hearty those days, which they ascribed to my being 'ignorant of the issues', and unable to share their sensitivities. Nothing seemed to grab hold of me, and once I found myself alone, the ersatz revolutionary fervour gradually fizzled out.

I was perhaps the permanent student that they refer to often, although I spent my time in public libraries more for physical warmth than for intellectual stimulation. Go and ask anybody who survived, they'll say that the Sixties was a great time to have been around, even if they look like total wrecks today.

I was glad that I had caught up with Colvin, even if he was proving not to be the same old Colvin. He looked content, as if he had nothing to grumble about. He probably guessed what I was thinking.

'Being a family man is not easy Baala. I think you are the lucky one.'

Ha! Now that was a total surprise. It may be that he is trying to play down his good fortune to make me feel less envious. Who knows?

'The worry is Baala, what sort of a world have we brought them up to inherit?' He spread his arms wide to indicate the children playing in the churchyard away from the adults congregated in the church hall.

'There was a time when you and I thought we could right the whole world, leave it a better place than we found it. Didn't we Baala?'

Colvin was becoming expansive, didactic – shades of the old Colvin. He even addressed me with the more affectionate shortened surname instead of my first name, which is Govind. He steered me to a trestle table at the back of the hall where the ladies were serving hot tea and coffee in paper cups. I asked for a coffee and had a muffin also pressed into my hand by a (not too) black girl wearing a smart trouser suit. She appeared to have made strenuous efforts to straighten her hair. She smiled indulgently showing perfect white teeth. Colvin tapped me on the back and sought my attention once again.

I surmised that he was about to expound some new ideology, since he was obviously no longer a full-blown Marxist.

'I am not all that religious as you probably already know. I won't conceal from you that I come here to network. Good for business, you know. Same reason I wear a well-pressed suit. Darwin explained it all. Survival requires camouflage.'

I thought he was digressing for some reason.

'For the ladies a chance to gossip.' I regretted it as soon as I said it.

'That's not PC, Baala!' Colvin almost shouted.

'Did you know that the woman who served you coffee – woman, mind you never girl – owns a medium-sized driving school? They are all here to network – also to show that they have a social conscience.'

'Yeah – so I am the down and out who happens to be the object of their charity today – is that it/?'

'Don't make it personal, Baala.'

That was enough to set me off.

'So all this is camouflage. All these massive social edifices we inherited have always been no more than bread and circuses of their time, waiting to be supplanted and transformed by capitalism and consumerism. Nothing personal – literally.'

Colvin took the bait.

'You could put it that way, except that both those 'isms' you mentioned are collective achievements, truly democratic and classless. You couldn't ascribe them to any particular philosopher or prophet, could you?'

Now the polemics were exactly like in the old days, although the content couldn't have been more dissimilar. Now my turn.

'I know. They are really not 'isms', but technologies. Technology, unlike pure academic science, is what makes for classlessness. Technology is in the public domain even allowing for patents and protectionism. When anybody can build a nuclear bomb these days, I wonder about your Darwinian survival. We humans as a species have made ourselves unfit to survive. Now, is this a sermon (since we are in a church) or – a Socratic dialogue (which I hope it is)?

The collection box came round just when Colvin had turned away, presumably to network.

I had cashed my Income Support Giro on Thursday, but had still managed to hang on to a few coins. I deposited a few in the box. Unusually for me I didn't get round to count them. Suddenly, I felt the seizure coming on. A condition I had developed, a few years back, after I had a joint or two followed by an unequal struggle with the strong arm of the law.

'Excuse me. Where's the toilet?'

Without waiting for an answer I ran and hid behind a gravestone at the back of the church, mainly to avoid any commiserations from Colvin.

I must have been out for the count for quite a long time, since when I woke up with an almighty headache, it was pitch dark and nobody was around. Nobody, that is, except for the gargoyles above in masks of Marx and Lenin, mocking me with their maniacal grimaces.

***

ENDGAME

We deem it progress
when the world has shrunk – is shrinking,
with more humans on the planet
less room for other species.
Is it survival of the fittest?
A premise that is questionable, equivocal.

We over-consume our resources,
oil, gas, coal, metallic ore:
crowd our space with mighty machines
in the air, sea, and on the ground.
We stockpile nuclear armaments
blind to the risk it entails:
hesitate replacing fossil fuel
with eco-friendly energy sources,
(sun, wind, water, and wave).

What are the options we have for our future?
The capitalist vision is for never-ending growth:
a high rate of return for every investment,
no ceiling envisaged at the end of this game.
Espionage provokes state belligerence,
a cyber-cloud of suspicion hangs over the planet.

A runaway world careers into oblivion.

LIFE EXPECTANCY

Frail and prey to infirmity in old age, yet,
grey cells and synapses active in the brain.
Remember the psychologists who wouldn't admit to 'mind'
Saying there is too much hidden behind this abstract noun
for it to be of any practical use,
relegating 'mind' to the metaphysical mumbo-jumbo
of 'How many angels could dance on a pinhead?'

Is it the mind/brain that is failing, when I can't remember
where I left my car-keys? An estimated forty-thousand
words in my vocabulary, ignoring the dormant extras of my native
tongue.
Where have I lodged them? Stored in millions of cells, I daresay;
though hard to draw from memory when sought.

Once I asked my wife for the term
for the ceramic installation adjacent to the WC
for ablutions not always requiring the shower, or bath.
Don't you know, it's the 'bidet', my wife prompted me;
support aligned well with domestic accord.

Human historical lifespan of three-score years and ten
stretches today into the nineties and hundreds;
a burden on the state, though politicians stay in office
well into their dotage, yet, they legislate
to set limits, and extend our pensionable age.

SALAD DAYS

I grab a colander from under the cupboard below the table top;
I've already laid a sheet of paper flat on the work surface.
Two red radishes topped and tailed are thrown into the colander first,
it now rests on that sheet of paper next to the chopping board.

A quartered red pepper goes in next, with half a red onion, small.
The Dutch cucumber need not be peeled, and an inch-long piece looks good;
though a Spanish *pepiño* requires peeling, as no one likes it's skin;
half a celery-stick needs clean shaving, not to be thrown in the bin.

The main ingredients of a salad are the bright green leaves of a lettuce.
A peeled tomato follows the carrots, either grated or sliced.
The lot is cut and chopped with a knife and washed inside a bowl;
eight green olives are quite enough, but sometimes we make it ten.

Half-a-lemon is squeezed over the mix; no need of pepper and salt,
with olive oil the main dressing, it augments our Mediterranean diet.

MOTHERLAND

However much you may have roamed the world
You could never forget your native land.
Like so many sheep steered back to the fold
Your thoughts return to where you played in the sand.

Breathtaking beauty of your island home
Often projected over the TV screen,
The majestic sweep of a 'Dagaba's dome
And the serene tranquillity of a rural scene.

'Goigama', the caste, but with no land of their own,
Parents, low paid, village teachers, strong
On moral convictions, as Buddhists, well-known
Guided us to distinguish right from wrong.

Wartime, hard-graft at boarding school,
English, the imperial language we had to learn
A path to advancement – the only tool,
And the means for a decent wage you could earn.

Gaining independence in Nineteen Forty-Eight
Paved the way for the traditionalists
Who rose to power promising greater weight
For the 'Sinhala only' of the nationalists.

The Tamil minority was up in arms
Favoured by the British when colonial masters;
The terrorist LTTE hadn't the slightest qualms
spawning suicide bombers causing deadly disasters.

An undeclared war of nearly thirty years
Spoiled the country's image and good name;
But Lanka's leaders assuaged our fears
By vanquishing the terrorists like hunted game.

Among the Tamils I had many close friends.
There's no reason, we could still find a way
For reconciliation, buck the negative trends,
Prevent antagonisms, build a healthier today.

AGE AND MOBILITY

Age and mobility do not go together.
More than ever, given the gift of longevity,
we elders desire and need to move around,
unsteady and wavering on our own two feet.
For a while, we resort to the staid walking stick,
or a friendly shoulder, then,- zimmer-frame,
wheel-chair – conveyances now seemingly ubiquitous.

Age and mobility do not go together.
But the passenger cruise and long-haul flight,
seduce senior citizens with spending power;
they can afford a taxi and the privately rented car,
instead of big city buses, trams, and the underground;
where space is earmarked for a clearly assigned role,
not always handed to the deserving soul.

When mother with baby-carriage asserted her right
to allocated space over a mobility-impaired man,
the courts wouldn't recognise a disabled pensioner's plight
but ruled that he await the next available ride.
Where age and mobility becomes a generational issue,
it's hard to determine the best course to pursue.

STELLAR ELLA

You came alive, rejuvenated, with the birth of your first grandchild,
our steadfast union had reached a plateau, an idyllic platonic state.
You always took care to avoid inhaling the body-odour of your mate,
but understood and forgave the reasons if he became irate.

Our junior, in your womb was winged from Africa to the East,
his older brother a tearful toddler. Now he presents his first-born baby,
long-awaited and prayed for. Ella comes too early to the feast
no bigger than the palm of your hand; she now blossoms and is feisty.

Happy and smiling you board the plane alone to reach little Ella
the proud *abuela* from Spain to England, a wee bit over a two-hour
flight,
unlike the marathon you once flew, to give birth to her dad in a
tropical isle.
London's East End, Olympic venue is Ella's home – at least for a while.

They idolise your ageless beauty, two summers short of your seventh
decade,
your kindness, grace and patience always captivates and enchants
them all,
family, friends and occasional guests arrive at a sun-drenched house in
Spain,
our lives have now become even more luminous with the burgeoning
wonder of stellar Ella.

CITRUS CHALLENGE

Of the two citrus trees we planted in our yard
the orange bore fruit given two years of growth;
the lemon grew tall, spread wide, stood guard,
but failed to yield fruit, reveal what it was worth.

Two bougainvillea, planted either side of the terrace,
bedecked the front porch; needed pruning all the time.
Showers of sparrow-droppings disfiguring the place,
left us no option but to slash them in their prime.

The barren citrus too, met the same unforgiving fate,
leaving us to nurture a two-foot toddler tree,
with hopes of ripe lemon at a not too distant date.
In a land famed for fruit, we needed them, fresh and free.

Watering the lemon plant, (we feared to excess),
gave us six lemons in the first year of its life.
No sign this year, even of limited success;
how long will it take for this fruit tree to become rife?

To our envy, the neighbours had a flourishing lemon tree,
Tall, in their front yard, any passer-by could see.
Of all the crazy things these gormless folk could do,
they chopped the citrus down saying it crowded their view!

A PENSIONER

An octogenarian - he moved to the retirement home
that promised all-year sun, blue sky, and sedate sea.

A grey, balding, and stooped figure,
his gait is far from firm as he walks.
Panoramic vistas, crushed-cardboard like hills,
frame the backdrop to his daily meanderings.
His dim and distorted memories mimic
the surrounding mountain range, hazily silhouetted against
the sparse, cloud-strewn sky.

A startled hare darts across the gravelly lane,
to join a squad of exuberant fellows, charging headlong
into the shrub, tails held high – quick flashes of white.
Transfixed, he stops to admire the moor-hen crossing his path,
her brood of chicks faithfully following in line.

The pomegranate grove sheds overripe fruit,
sighs with relief, longing for hibernation.
Artichokes, green and bright, proudly claim eagerness to be picked
and make room for a different crop.

Rebirth and renewal, the pattern of seasons,
choreograph the remaining years, (months and days), for this old man.

THE EMPEROR OF EXMOOR

He lived too long and needed to be culled
the Emperor of Exmoor, the nine-foot tall stag;
his burgeoning fame may have left him lulled
into believing that he was invulnerable to be bagged

for a magnificent dinner which would proudly enable
visiting dignitaries at Her Majesty's table
to feast on the flesh of this royal beast.
No – the stag was too old to be relished as meat.

His horns were what the stalker had in mind
as a trophy to excel the best of its kind;
the emperor succumbed to a well-aimed shot
from a licensed assassin who felled him on the spot.

The Emperor, Pharaoh-like, partial to incest
endangered continuing survival of the fittest;
trounced by a young buck in a recent wrestling match
his reign had just ended as lord of the patch.

HALLOWEEN DAY

I feel fine, though my blood-sugar is high
Checked after a swig of cold water and lime,
Porridge for breakfast, with raisins and prunes.
An oscine bird sings, (NOT obscene, I groan!),
Outside the window in "full-throated ease"
Perched on a bougainvillea, lovingly grown
By my dear wife which graces the terrace,
A playground for sparrows, to butterflies a maze.

I switch on the desktop, no e-mails do I see
The telly draws me next to the Saturday morning show
Of classical concerts on the Spanish Channel, y'know;
I am still in my sarong; hope the neighbours won't be
Curious 'bout a garment made fashionable by Beckham
Being worn by a man who once lived in Peckham.

Outside I hear the wind-chimes calling
And hoist the sunshade for an hour's cogitating.
Someone at the gate: 'Where have you been
To say you didn't know - today 's Halloween?

FANI

Some years ago she was a very young girl
shy and engaging, lacking conversation
as her native tongue was different from mine.
Nor had we, a common second language;
yet, she sought to convey the quiet concern
owed to a stranger in a foreign land
with her sweet, considerate, amenable, mien.

Six years passed, with marriage and motherhood,
two babes in her care, still working for a living,
behind the Council information desk.
Smiles her welcome, with eyes deep blue,
a sight so appealing and distinguished.
As a woman fulfilled in her feminine role,
she makes the pueblo proud, one of its daughters to be.

FAIRGROUND

Life is but a gaudy fairground
of childish expectations, chancy attainments,
and, wildly wayward disappointments.

Achievements propel us roller coaster high;
failure drives one to hide away and cry.

Most of us who've come for the ride are mournful also-rans.
A few happy souls, favoured and feisty, climb the victory dais;
some who reach the perilous peak come crashing down to earth
others are accorded deserving honours, even after their death.

Within a very short lifespan, we suffer many ups and downs;
media forces into our homes the world's misery and dross.
Striving can be laudable, and so is accepting one's lot;
shoulders against the grindstone, or else, - go smoke pot.

Sisyphus sights his nemesis as a lotus-eating ethos.

WATER

Water, wonderful, born of gases, sharing oxygen with air
Odourless, tasteless, colourless marvel, translucently clever;
Man created electric light to emulate the sun for a dare
But no invention could replace water, there's no substitute - ever.

Fire evokes frantic fear, the deepest respect, and awe
While water prevails in every contest being fought between the two
Fire helps cold water to boil, as a friend, and never as a foe
You may drink with confidence; it's bound to be a fine brew.

"Water, water, everywhere but not a drop to drink"
The Mariner knew that oceans covered a greater part of the earth.
Worthless even for washing up dishes lying dirty in the kitchen sink
Yet caring clouds pour refreshing rain, to give the rivers new birth.

Drought and dearth of water, they say, could trigger the Third
World War
When all the rivers are dammed, diverted, and inadvertently drained
All for the sake of parochial power; the cost is in trillions or more,
While the landscape lies denuded, bare - as if it had never rained.

Water, wonderful, born of gases, the elixir of life,
Superannuated by human stupidity to become the cause of strife.

THE RECKONING

Have we not witnessed two centuries of hate
Unspeakable horrors, on land and on seas,
Forced Democracy down on her knees
With barbaric massacres and mindless waste?
Yet blinding Hatred brooks no debate;
Intellect revered, but Wisdom and Peace
Held to ransom by plutocrats obese.
Undermined, Faith flees, carries no weight
While despots, demagogues, harangue the masses
Slaves to gadgetry and consumer greed,
Mammon dictates with none to intercede
Over a planet denuded of natural resources.
　　　Blithely blinkered in rose-tinted glasses
　　　We ignore the reckoning – it fast approaches.

THE MINSTREL

If you had heard him singing beneath the trees
an environmental ditty to the accompaniment of bees,
would you have guessed that this weary wanderer,
an excrescence of Empire, of subject race,
a rootless yokel, had at last found a voice?
You may conclude that he had no choice.

Straining synapses in his bicameral brain,
ogling at horrors on the television screen,
massacres, mayhem, pathological frenzy,
suffering most deeply world's existential pain;
while economic meltdown plagues nations at peril,
he weaves narratives with a pitiful refrain.

He sings not for his supper, but for the approval
of a few, and entertains them as a personable clown.
an oddity, perhaps, never the toast of the town,
nor a migrant bird that flies in formation
with purpose and direction, hard-wired or learnt,
he's happy to meander, dreamlike in a swoon.

His songs are few, echoing the loneliness of his heart,
a lyrical glissando, trans-mutated into art.
Oak-aged, barrel-seasoned, an authentic voice,
would you concede that he had no choice?

STILLNESS BY THE SHORE

Evening of life when the days are long
unleashes the power of the poet within.
Somnolent siestas are a summer's blessing;
gentle wind softens proud visage of the sun;
static clouds whiten the soft azure sky,
pine forests, green, stretch away from the sea.

Rainbow-hued parasols on promenade by the sea,
its lake-like serenity, soothing and blessing
a host of sea-bathers encouraged to lie long
in languid waters treading sea-weed within.
Still, there are those who'd rather be in the sun
imbibing vitamins from a benevolent sky.

Thunder and lightning, rain down from the sky;
when the sky is benign who doubts it a blessing?
While turbulent skies mirror storms within,
humans vacillate, unlike the constant sun;
tangled in turmoil like the rollers of the sea,
lives ephemeral, not seen for very long.

Thriving on mud, sleek seaweed grows long.
Bathers swim buoyant in the supple, shallow sea;
they are not bothered by the boisterous sun
believing its rays but a bounteous blessing.
When the weather is fine, you see a smiling sky
pampering, flattering - inducing peace within.

The classical sestina, unlocks the poet within.
To write a pleasing poem won't take one that long;
glowing poetic conceits raise spirits to the sky
carried by the summer breeze inspired by the sun.
Clothed in a conch-shell cast out to sea,
'Ode Less Travelled' is the guide, and a blessing.

To live life in the moment is an unmitigated blessing,
no striving or seeking, for the goal is within.
Use the instant now, however short or long
observing the glow of the serene setting sun,
orb of eternal splendour, majestic in the sky;
herald of day's departure over horizon and sea.

Envoi
The world **within** wakes to an exhilarating **sky;**
while the imperious **sun** bestows its kindest **blessing**
on a calm benign **sea,** all summer day **long.**

ST PETERSBURG

They had not stopped calling it Leningrad long
When I strode the streets of St Petersburg;
As the November snow gently caressed my feet
I reached the Monument of German defeat.

The Kirov Ballet and the Hermitage
Deeply impressed me, as the Nevsky barge,
Reminders of her once glittering past
When Prince Mishkin headed the Dostoevskian cast.

Tolstoy, Chekov, Turgenev and others
Are read and venerated, while no one bothers
With Lenin or Stalin, who vanquished the nobles
While promising to redistribute the country's roubles.

A mere three days happened all too soon
To end my sojourn of the Russian town
All I brought home was a matryoshka doll
Embodying the depths of the Russian soul.

SPANISH WARMTH

Genuine unforced smiles and looks, from youthful check-out staff
A daily feature in villages and towns in the less-harried south of Spain,
Our attempts to speak Español is valued; it does not raise a laugh
At supermarkets or roadside shops there's nothing for us to complain.

A third world country is an epithet heard, but the British have got it
wrong
Spain is far more advanced in medicine, in horticulture she excels;
The building boom with 'land grab' laws, thankfully didn't last long
So this is the time to pick up a bargain, to choose a property that sells.

Wine is plentiful and bodegas thrive with a Rioja on every table
There's hardly any drunken behaviour heard of in cafes, restaurants or
bars;
The streets are calm with peace-loving folk, the young being ready and
able
To remain dignified and decorous, while driving home in their cars.

People retired here are taken up with the easy and happy camaraderie
For the warmth of climate, leisurely lifestyle that only this country
affords
Spaniards are given to verbal jousting; they really know how to be
merry
But to praise Carmen, Jose and Lourdes, there simply are no words.

SCRIBE

Day after day, he sits on the terrace
surveying the landscape of his unfulfilled dreams.

Reality is bleak – nothing is built under power-carrying pylons
except for a children's park with see-saw, slide and swings.

Women work hard, despite the September sun
wearing protective gear of broad-brimmed hats
and long-sleeved *camisetas*. Chattering gaily
they clear the land, of parched, prickly, shrubs
behind imposing, though empty commercial units.

How did he earn his keep all his adult years?
By some sleight of hand, and crafty subterfuge –
it clearly now appears.

For he has no skill, other than to spill
verbiage on the page with an imaginary quill.
If truth be our gauge, he has time to kill.

RAIN IN SPAIN

October rain
Visits us with a vengeance
When least expected;
For baking July - searing August
Had left us wondering
Whether thunder and lightening
Aren't the foes we had forgot?

The roads are turned into torrents and rivers
Not quite what's expected by holiday drivers.
A round of golf even a dip in the sea,
Are denied to folk who can well afford the fee;
We do not see the best of Spain
When scurrying for shelter from the October rain.

Settled in the Costas we are expatriates here,
Lured by the sun, sea, sand, sangria, and beer.
Some of us are resident - others come and go
Seeing the seasons change with temperatures high and low.

Those who fought forest fires earlier this year
Welcome the October rain, to them most dear.

MY TEACHER

She never cried at her husband's death
Whom she had nurtured in sickness and in health;
Her presence in Paris - no romantic dream,
But a necessity occasioned by his treatment regime.

Learned, cultured, a historian and scholar
She edits his posthumous books with flair.
A teacher of English, acclaimed everywhere
From London to Paris, her students do care.

Witty and alert in her tenth decade,
She teaches with love, no cost to her charges;
They reach their goals, and spring to the aid
Of a lady of true grit who asks no favors.

My dream came true with her arrival in Spain
One week with us, unlikely to visit again,
Leaving fond memories that will never fade
A lady so special, she's queen of her domain.

Her generosity is such that she feels the need to repay
Kindnesses shown in the smallest way;
Will we ever see such a fine lady again?
A lady of true grit, queen of her domain.

THE VILLAGE BAR

The ground-floor of a terraced house
in a narrow side street,
where homely fare is freshly cooked;
Vino de mesa, clear and cool to taste,
no frills, but simple crudités.

The salad is green and crisp to bite,
aceite de oliva, generously spread
on barra pan, an honest local bread.
Allioli at times, and chutney on the house,
a lonely prawn perhaps, with a gherkin on the side.

'Tis no surprise that soup follows close;
will there be room for the hearty main course?
No fear, we are served fresh pollo and fish,
cerdo, if you prefer, and conejo, your wish,
they fill the plate lavishly that veggies complete.

Elsewhere the food may be cheap even more,
but, add the price of bebidas, and the bills will soar.
So who cares for show, and frivolous fanfare
when good food is plentiful at our friendly village bar?

TODAY IN THE NEWS

Mothers and newborn prematurely die, at a state of the art maternity ward,
Miners, meeting demand for coal, perish trapped deep down in colliery pits;
A home appliance improperly wired, explodes, killing a sleeping brood.
The White House, in the United States, was built entirely by the labour of slaves.

A fugitive killer who escaped prison is caught on the run after forty-one years;
A human vegetable wanting to die is denied the right by the nation's Courts,
Asylum seekers defy a ruling that they should be deported to the land of their birth.
A little known fact in history is that the White House was built by America's slaves.

Neighbours are kind, when they come round, to paint our parapets a brilliant white,
All they ask for is a nice cup of tea, enjoying a break sitting out on the terrace;
Absent on holiday in a cold climate, what a pleasant surprise for the returning spouse!
Liberty pronounced an inalienable right while blacks were building the US White House.

SURROGATE SON

The boy was birthed by Caesarean section,
full term spent in his host mother's womb;
his origin, exotic, was a laboratory feat.
Random female egg, fertilised by the sperm
of a Spanish male donor (or, so it is averred);
a treatment denied in the land of her birth.

Many years dormant, frozen and sealed,
a healthy embryo grows, once implanted
surrogate, in the belly of a fifty-year–old.
The lady, a spinster, of charm and intellect,
has claims to a flourishing, professional practice
in London's affluent, St John's Wood.

With dark shiny hair and olive-coloured skin,
the boy, now three, spends a summer break in Spain.
His mother, impervious to his obscure genetic past,
bows down and caters to his every passing whim.
'Uno, dos, tres', he readily sings in Spanish;
one senses that the world will soon be at his feet.

SUMMER'S HERE

Born, bred, and browned in the tropics
for me, every day was sparkling summer,
save for the occasional spare monsoon
when thunder and lightning smote our land;
sure, the sun smirked behind every shower,
and warmth wouldn't be long denied
to those who ploughed the paddy fields
with gratitude for Nature's munificence.
They fed a faithful farming flock,
whose simple needs were met in abundance.

As I grew up and moved to the West
encountered hailstorm, snowfall and sleet;
the sun appeared a shade too shy
to come out strong, until July.
Then everyone spoke of nothing but the weather
clamouring jubilantly 'Summer's here!';
with raw skin exposed, shamefully bare,
spread out supine, daring the sun.

Where a well-tanned hide is conspicuously rare,
I thank heaven for an in-built one.

MY ROUND

Days of the week, pretty much the same
On the terrace sipping beer or wine, never tea,
Evening draws close last innings of the game,
When Levantine breezes blow cold from the sea.
Where in the world would you-and I rather be?
In a Mediterranean villa, freehold to our name.
Friends made here, prove rather good company.
No rush-hour traffic – we're thrilled that we came,
Though traffic on the Internet will keep us very busy.
Voipcheap and Skype, we could well pick and choose
With whom to speak, (from where), when to use.
Who could have dreamt that life was this easy?

Given a lifetime of toil, us pensioners have found
A lifestyle to savour – 'Cheers – it's my round!'

LOCAL FIESTA

Historic church, distant from the town, in homage
to the Virgin enthroned, stands on a hill.
The Queens and Ladies of Honour, visibly
the prettiest in town, are crowned and paraded with paeans
from the powerful. Bountiful bouquets, floral sprays,
and framed endorsements, are showered on the chosen.

Town folk (expats included) sip wine, or beer in bars and terraces
all around the square. Guests sit in rows of plastic pews neatly
arranged
before a televised stage and podium. Children play, bursting their
balloons
among adoring parents. Pubescent girls gyrate on stage to canned
music.
Rockets and exploding fire-crackers fiercely announce
the resilience of a pueblo, flourishing amidst the crisis, braving all
odds.

Ten days and nights of free-for-all fun, scheduled to end on
'dia de la morera' (mulberry tree day), a day set apart, (I quote)
'for everybody to do as they please!'

LIFE-SPACE

Please grant me space, I want to live
freed from past failure. A few forgotten
triumphs, thinly glimpsed, remain shining
like polished armour; hardly a crusading knight
defending honour, faith or creed.

Instead, taken-for-granted services offered
to fellow humans for paltry recompense.
Sequel to long languishment in lowly work, inducing
contempt of others in looks, words and deeds.
Wedded, with dutiful mate sharing the happy burden,
Earning a wage, bringing up children, now flown the nest.

Recollections - claws of ragged acrimony, grate over
past-inflicted sores. Let me bury these now and forever;
find space here, where I want to live
in harmony and peace,
having no higher powers to please.

JAZZ BAND

Swept away by the jazz-band magic
at dusk, sitting in the Reina Sofia park,
spread out with legroom - no poky theatre here.
Glad I coaxed *mi mujer* to come over.
Fourth of July, any significance in that?
For our American cousins - a holiday, in fact.

We've special affection for Guardamar del Segura,
our first port-of–call on moving to this land.
A children's fair swings faint in the distance
as the drummer insists on his exuberant solo,
with help from the rough-throated backing group,
a pride of peacocks by the triple pond.

The sun hasn't set, even late at ten;
men in short-sleeved shirts escort their women
vying with each other in seasonable dress;
where can one feel such warmth, but in Spain?

Pine trees silhouetted against the gloaming sky,
clouds afloat, while the crescendo soars,
four in the ensemble, no wind instruments,
a keyboard, guitar; string, and percussion.

It's still not quite dark, but the stars are out,
a sparkling canopy over a jubilant jazz band
enthralling a non-paying, appreciative crowd,
at Guardamar del Segura, this historical town.

DEMO-CRAZY

Democracy ensures that the jobless poor gets a hand-out called the dole;
though politicians are aware that it creates an indefensible hole
in a country's finances when they haven't the means other than to borrow
from every source, as if there is no accounting for the 'morrow.

How do you square such profligacy with the triumph of capitalism
when we are lulled into believing that it had totally trounced communism?

The West is forced to sell or sink while the Chinese dump these days;
with bombing raids in faraway lands costing trillions, - who pays?
Energy sources are depleted and fossil fuel cost the earth
to extract and to distribute, though there is no 'fracking' dearth

of many other sources of energy to redeem a planet ravaged by pollution.
Can wind and solar power prevail, though some prefer a nuclear solution?

Phrases are coined very aptly and glibly like 'being economical with the truth'.
Media giants, trans-nationals rule – provoke at your peril their wrath; with concealment and cyber espionage, instruments of state and trade, fake news promote Brexit and Trump - we are manipulated – be afraid.

Democracy hobbles, a pathetic figure, in a shadowy Orwellian world; the rich (one percent) gets the right to rule with no banners ever unfurled.

CURTAIN CALL

Musings on more than a decade of retirement;
no report card scribble: 'could've done better'.
Old put-downs, praise, blame, and shame,
all the same now. Nothing would jolt
the diurnal cadence of living and ageing.
Riding the bike, dip in the sea, few lengths in the pool,
bringing wayward blood-sugar back to heel.
No excess, or excuse needed, for a glass or two with friends.

Eye-sight, reflexes, tested and judged
more than adequate for driving around
planning to return before dark - unless, to pick up
or drop off family and friends at the airport –
not forgetting the local fiesta, musical show, flamenco night,
costing next to nothing.

Life's purpose affirmed in every diurnal act
presages loud hosannas before the curtain falls.

MARKET FORCES (ONE ACT PLAY)

Cast in order of appearance:

> **David Brown**
> **Susan Brown**
> **Ms Katy Bond**
> **Indian couple** (very brief appearance)
> **Alan**

Scene 1

> David and Susan Brown's home in a suburb of Greater London. It is late morning, Sunday. And the couple are in their bedroom getting dressed.

David: (*apologetically*) Susan, I know you keep telling your friends that I don't take you out often enough. Now, here's a whole evening at Midtown Hotel. Drinks on the house – says here. (*He rustles and shows a paper*) What more do you want?

Susan: Oh yea! On the house! Anything for free and you jump at it like a … what was it you used to say? … Ah yes. Pavlov's dog.

David:	What are you on about? This is a prize I won. Yes... A Prize, all due to my talent for words and years spent as a teacher of psychology. A good motivational jingle was what they wanted, and that's exactly what they got. Here I am with the second prize, probably missing the first by a whisker. Here's my prize-winning ditty. *(He recites)* 'Tommy the Texan fancies he's a pirate, Call him a Yankee, and he gets irate. If his ancestors had their own way, Blacks (didn't use the 'n' word) would still be cott'n pickin' today!' *(repeats without the exegesis)* How's that!
Susan:	Fantastic! You ought to have won the first prize. This is only a free drink and the **promise** *(emphasis)* of a holiday abroad. You deserve to have won the £10,000 first prize.
David:	Never mind darling. Ten thousand quid wouldn't have been enough for me to ditch my astronomically well-paid job teaching evening classes in A' Level psychology. Plenty more years before retirement to sun, sea, sand, and sangria.
Susan:	*(Thoughtful)* Now I am having second thoughts about going to this, David. Isn't there a general scare about all this pressure selling? Time-share and stuff like that!
David:	No darling. What could they sell us? We have no dinero. No investments, shares, savings in the Bank. Just about enough to meet the monthly mortgage payments and to put our daily bread on the table. Everybody knows we live from day to day, hand to mouth. They can't sell us anything. This paper *(touching his pocket)* says in black and white that I am guaranteed a prize – a free holiday – either they

give us what they promise, or we say – bye, bye. Won't do us any harm just being there.

Susan: (*distant*) Hope so.

David: Oh come on! You always fantasised about the West End at night. To have a peek at whatever was going on in Soho.

Susan: …and you never bothered to take me there.

David: So, here's your chance. We'll get there a bit early and have s snoop around.

Susan: Okey dokey. But I must be back by 11.30 the latest. I missed Big Brother all last week. Luckily I videoed some of it. If I don't watch tonight, I'll never have the time.

David: Yea. Ok. (*reflecting*) How quickly the weekend goes! That reminds me, I must get out the old 'Hierarchy of Needs' OHT for the Tuesday class.

Susan: Oh your speciality! Teaching motivation to kids. They don't need these abstruse theories. All anyone wants today is money, money, money!!!

David: Sex more than money, my lot.

Susan: They are only kids aren't they? (*musing*) Nobody chasing after you, I hope.

David: They're not all kids…. (*suddenly picking up on the question*) Oh dozens! They just can't keep their hands off older men, these dolly birds.

Susan: Oh shut up and hurry up. By the way, you'll have to get yourself a travel card. I can use my season ticket.

David: Now don't get off the topic. What's the attraction of Soho for you? Is it the sex shows and shops or just its reputation. Come on, I am ready.

Susan: Well. Nothing like finding out what you are missing, see how the other half lives.

David: Come to think of it, I might find their sales methods interesting. Get a few pointers on how I can improve – bring up to date - my motivation lesson. Oh Maslow, dear Maslow!

Susan: Got the keys? Come on then.

(They exit stage with the sound of the front door being shut)

CURTAIN

Scene 2

Off stage a man's voice calling, *"Mr and Mrs Ahuliwala"*. This is repeated twice with rising inflection at the end. Shuffling noises off stage.

Male voice   Mr and Mrs Ahuliwala, this is your holiday
(*(off stage)*):   consultant for the evening. Miss Bond. (*an attractive young lady appears on stage*)

(Indian man and woman enter and speak with marked accents)

Indian woman: *(plaintively)* But ... but ... we only go to India on holiday.

Indian man: *(shaking head from side to side)* We can't afford to go anywhere else.

Man (*entering*):	Yes. Yes. India, Thailand, Hong Kong, Malaysia, we have holidays all over the world. Won't hurt you to look ... and ... listen... (*He escorts them off stage with faint protests from the Indian couple*)
Ms Bond:	(*Shuffling papers*) Mr and Mrs Brown? Hello!

(Susan and David *enter from off-stage*)

Susan:	That's us. Our turn.
Ms Bond:	Nice to meet you (*shakes hands*) I am Katy, The holiday consultant.
David and Susan:	Pleased to meet you.
Ms Bond:	Come over. Come this way. Have you been here before?
David:	No. First time.
Ms Bond:	You are here for the free holiday, of course. There will be just a half-hour presentation before you'll be awarded your prize. Hope you enjoy it.
David:	(*surprised*) Presentation! Presentation of what?
Ms Bond:	(*appearing breathless with every sentence*) We are the biggest and best known holiday homes organization in Europe. We are affiliated to the largest holiday home exchange organization in the world based in the United States. We have access to over 2000 holiday resorts all over the world. Come to think of it, we are the first to get into the holiday home business in Eastern Europe. So, if you are with us, you will enjoy the biggest choice of holiday homes for the rest of your life which you can exchange

year in and year out. And, you pay so little for the privilege. You will be the envy of your friends. Exciting isn't it? You can hear and see more on the video in a minute.

David: (*turning to Susan*) What have we got ourselves in for? We don't need all this. (*turning to Ms Bond*) We have only come to claim the prize. (*Struggles to take out the piece of paper from his jacket pocket*) (*Sounds of scraping chairs and buzz of conversation off stage*)

Ms Bond: That's right. You are with us for the evening. I've got your forms here. Would you like some coffee … or a drink?

David: Ah! Drinks … I thought….

Ms Bond: (*quickly*) Soft drinks, of course.

David and   (*together*) No thanks. We've just had coffee.
Susan:

Ms Bond: Do sit yourselves down. I'll find you seats. There's more than thirty seats already taken. Good show!

(*Curtain comes down momentarily but opens to reveal a seated stage audience Ms Blond escorts Susan and David to two seats among the audience*)

Alan: (*the man whose voice was heard earlier addressing the seated group*) Before we begin the serious business of the day – that is, the holiday you've all come here for – tell me, would anyone here like to have something for nothing?

(*Awkward silence*)

Alnn: Okay. There are no mugs here. That's for sure. You are all a very intelligent lot. Right, who would like this picnic set worth £20 for 50 pence? *(continued silence)* *(Man pretending to be amazed)* No one, how about one pound then?

Woman: *(from back of the stage)* Oh yes please … Where's the catch?

Alan: No catch. You demonstrated that there is no place you can get something for nothing in this world. But… but, you can always get a bargain, something very cheap. Let's say that's market forces working. You can get things almost for nothing – but not often enough. You must know where and when you can get a bargain. That's where we come in. We are in the know. Here we are, you just bought a £20 worth of goods for a mere quid. You just proved it.

Woman: *(breathless)* Thank you very much.

Alan: *(patronisingly)* You know you could have got this fifty percent cheaper if only you were quick enough and brave enough to realise what was happening. Keep that in mind for the rest of the evening … all of you.

David: *(aside sotto voce to Susan)* All this is pre-arranged you know. She is a plant.

Alan: Once only, who wants this bone china, Charles and Diana inscribed mug for two quid? They are no longer in production. Collector's item. *(Most of the audience including Susan but not David shout* ME, ME)

| **Alan:** | Right – to the gentleman in the blue jumper. (*While handing over the mug and collecting money, the chime of a bell is heard*) I apologise for having to stop now, but we have the rare opportunity of viewing a video presentation of one of the greatest holiday home developments of the century. Let me introduce you to our hostess today Ms Katy Bond. |

(In the background the voice of a well-known TV personality of the Eighties is heard enthusiastically introducing a holiday golf resort and retirement homes in Andalusia, Spain. This fades)

David:	This lark is not to my liking. Why the hell would anyone in their right minds want to buy a 50p mug for two quid!
Susan:	Really grand. (*obviously referring to what she now sees on the TV screen*) I wouldn't mind a kitchen like that.
David:	(*not bothering*) Grand? I prefer to call the whole thing weird.
Susan:	You would! Wouldn't you? What sort of an idiot are you?
Alan:	Anybody here like what they see? You are all interested in holidays – that's why you are here today. Am I right? (*Chorus of approving noises*)

And, how much do you think a five-star accommodation like that'd cost you to own – for your exclusive use all-year round? (*noises and murmurs*)

You don't know! I'll tell you. Four hundred grand at least, not to speak of stamp duty, lawyer's fees, service charges, local authority rates, maintenance etc. etc. However, if fifty of you get together you would have this pile for practically nothing. Say, there's a round fifty weeks in a year, allowing for two weeks closed for maintenance. You would only need £8,000 each to collectively own that magnificent mansion in Hungary. Maybe a few bob extra between you for rates and upkeep. Hang on a minute, I must stress that since you are all not going to be using all four self-contained suites in that mansion, for one suite each, you pay only £2,000. Getting better and better isn't it? Now, that is still not the whole story. Some of you will want to take a holiday in high summer; others may prefer spring or autumn, while still others may want a winter break. So, again deciding among yourselves, some will pay a little more for the high season, and others less. Even Steven, All depends on the demand. If more of you want summer, then the price goes up. If only a few ask for a less attractive period of the year, then they become much cheaper. Now, we have here a breakdown of what an average family spends on their annual holiday. *(A flipchart is seen)* It's a staggering £3,500. Goes up with inflation every year. With our arrangement your holiday is inflation-proofed throughout your natural life. Once you pay the relatively small agreed sum, it's yours for the next 25 years. You may not want to take a holiday every year. You may have other important things in your life to attend to, a wedding, and, God forbid, a funeral. We understand all that. You can bank your week or two weeks and use it at a later date. You can exchange your week for another in a different resort in a different country – in fact anywhere in the civilized world. There's so much you can do once you own that week or two. We are affiliated to a world renowned holiday resort exchange organization. It is all beautifully explained in our brochure. Copies with your consultant Katy Bond. *(Speeding up the patter)* There are special offers just for today. I hope you'll grasp this unique opportunity with both hands. There's no time for shilly-shallying. These properties go like hot cakes. Don't forget you are here by personal invitation. No one else will have the chance that you are offered today. Today, there are special deals, deferred payment schemes, loans etc etc. So, there's no excuse; get the details from Katy. *(More slowly)* D'you know, you are very privileged people. I envy you. Honestly. *(Applause)*

Ms Bond: *(to David and Susan)* So, how did you like the presentation.

David:	Good, very good, but we are not here to buy a holiday home. We are only interested in the free holiday, the prize I am supposed to have won.
Ms Bond:	Yes, yes. All in good time. May I ask, what do you do for a living?
David:	*(exasperated)* Look, it's all in the form we filled in. I teach psychology and my wife is in admin - civil service. We want to get back home fairly early, if you don't mind. My wife wants to watch a program on TV. Not much different from what you got here. Pandering to the basest instincts – pure greed. I don't know what she sees in all this, but we must get away soon. Otherwise ... big trouble.
Ms Bond:	I understand you wanting to get a move on, Sir. Alan will see you in a minute.
David:	Besides, the West End is no place to hang around at night. Not these days.
Alan:	*(shuffling a sheaf of papers)* Let me see your documentation. Right, according to the code number here, as you can see, which matches this one here, you have won a two-week free accommodation at Belliake, in one of our best resorts, the five-star Crown Head Don Quixote Inn. Now this is only free accommodation, not with full board, ok?
Susan:	What kind of prize is that? It can't be a self-catering pad. This is supposed to be a posh hotel with in-house restaurant facilities.
Alan:	Yes. Yes. Free breakfast, but you will have to have at least one main meal a day at the Don Quixote Restaurant, and, of course you pay for it.

David:	Then, what about the flight? I mean how are we supposed to get there?
Alan:	Entirely your responsibility. You could fly. You could sail. You could drive, or walk! (*Motioning with hand to indicate flying, sailing, driving and walking*)
Susan:	(*riled*) Bollocks! A fine second prize. Would be cheaper to go camping. Our usual holiday mode.
David:	We've wasted our time here haven't we? A damned good lesson. Let's call it a day. Let's go home.
Alan:	Look! What made you come here today? Isn't it because you are fed up with the same old way of holidaying year in and year out, and are interested in upgrading your holiday lifestyle. Don't you deserve a more luxurious time in a hotel suite?
David:	We also know only too well the limits of our financial resources. We are quite satisfied with the lifestyle we have.
Susan:	(*sulking, sotto voce*) Speak for yourself. I quite like some of what they are offering.
Alan:	Just the point I am trying to get across. You wouldn't be doing the same thing every year if you can do better with the same resources. Once you buy into our scheme you fix the amount of your annual outlay on holidays to what you paid today, bought at a very reasonable price. A price that is totally inflation-proof.
David:	(*sounding alarmed*) Anyway, I won't sign anything until I've checked things with a solicitor.
Alan:	You don't know a good deal when you see it, do you? You say you teach psychology?

David:	*(feigning anger)* What's that got to do with it?
Alan:	Oh! You are a tough one. You know, I once followed evening classes in psychology. Didn't stay the course, otherwise I'd have got my A' Levels by now.
David:	Never too late. You can come to my class. Tuesday evenings 7.00 to 9.00. I'll give you the details. New course starts September.
Alan:	*(ignoring)* So you see everything has its time. We cannot keep this offer open until you have consulted your solicitor. Ours is a standard package. It has been approved by a panel of international lawyers. In fact, I can get our Managing Director to have a word with you, if you like. Luckily he is here with us today. I am sure he could explain the legal side of things to your satisfaction.
David:	Look! I don't want to talk to your MD. We don't want to buy timeshare. Do you understand, once and for all?
Alan:	Tut, tut. Timeshare? We don't use such terms here, this is just plain holiday ownership. You know you can sell or transfer the title deeds to the property. It is an investment. Are you sure you want to pass this up? You wouldn't have this chance again in your lifetime, believe me.
David:	*(voice rising)* No. no. I don't want any of it. If you have no prize holiday which doesn't involve our having to pay for meals and flights, then please let us go.

Alan:	No. You can't just leave like that. Do yourself a favour. Please talk to our MD. … Look, why are you being so difficult? It's a measly two grand we are talking about. Usually, at current prices it costs £3,500 for a family holiday in the peak season.
David:	Oh yes. This is a peak experience, I must say. Never had one like this before.
Alan:	What? What? What's that?
David:	Motivational psychology. In the Maslovian hierarchy, peak experiences and self-actualisation are ranked among the highest and most valued rung of human motivation. But, we have to satisfy our basic needs first. Our basest needs, I should say.
Susan:	(*having impatiently waited in the background*) Getting very late. No time for psychology lessons David. Come on. We've got to get home!
Alan:	Of course. But not before you've had your present.
David/Susan:	(*in unison*) Present? What present?
Alan:	Since you have turned down the prize holiday offer, and our rules don't allow us to let our guests leave empty handed, you are awarded a 12-month supply of weekly tickets to the clip joint – I mean the Strip Club in Dean Street. Round the corner. Thank you for coming today. (*Sounds of an on-stage audience applauding*).
Susan:	Get off!!! Who the hell do you think we are?
David:	Hang on a minute Susan, this is exactly what I want; to motivate my students. The week's best essay gets a ticket to the Strip Club. Let me grab them with both hands.

Thank you, thank you, the best reinforcement I've had in a long time.

Maslow, dear Maslow.

Susan: Salivating like Pavlov's pup, aren't you!!!

David: (*grabbing the tickets from Alan, runs off-stage*) Cheerio! Bye, bye, Adios!

CURTAIN

Lightning Source UK Ltd.
Milton Keynes UK
UKHW010602010519
341917UK00001B/30/P